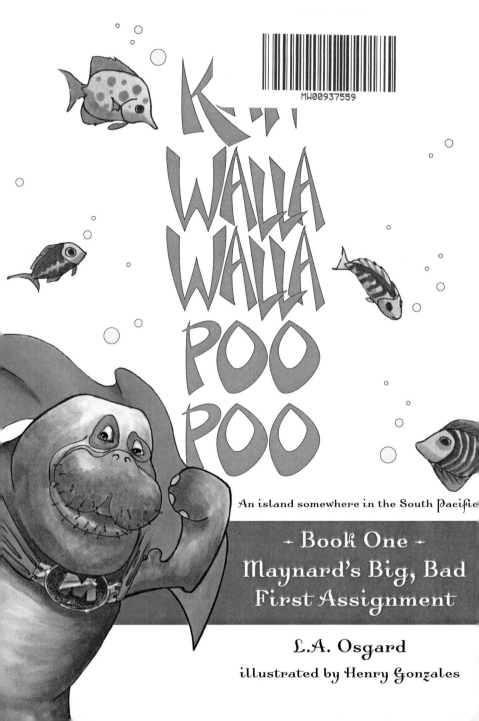

KAHWALLAWALLAPOOPOO, BOOK ONE: MAYNARD'S BIG, BAD FIRST
ASSIGNMENT

1405 SW 6th Avenue • Ocala, Florida 34471 • Phone 800-814-1132 • Fax 352-622-1875
Website: www.atlantic-pub.com • Email: sales@atlantic-pub.com
SAN Number: 268-1250

Names: Osgard, Lisa, author.
Title: Kawallawallapoopoo :Maynard's Big, Bad First Assignment / by Lisa Osgard.
Description: Ocala, Florida : Atlantic Publishing Group, Inc, [2018] |Series:
    Kawallawallapoopoo adventure ; [book №1] | Summary: Maynard, the Mystical Guiding
    Manatee, takes Jake to Kawallawallapoopoo Island, in hopes he can persuade the king to
    lift his ban on baseball but first, Jake wants his timid cousin, Kacey, to join him.
Identifiers: LCCN 2017055493 (print) | LCCN 2018000468 (ebook) | ISBN
    9781620235157 (ebook) | ISBN 9781620235140 (alk. paper) | ISBN 1620235145
    (alk. paper)
Subjects: CYAC: Manatees--Fiction. | Baseball--Fiction. | Adventure and adventurers--Fic-
    tion. | Cousins--Fiction. | Islands--Fiction.
Classification: LCC PZ7.1.O843 (ebook) | LCC PZ7.1.O843 Kaw 2018 (print) |DDC
    [Fic]--dc23
LC record available at https://lccn.loc.gov/2017055493

Printed in the United States

PROJECT MANAGER: Danielle Lieneman
INTERIOR LAYOUT: Nicole Sturk

Dedication

Mom, this book I dedicate to you.

You passed away far too young and with far
too many stories unwritten. You were practically
world-famous for your correspondence to friends and
family and everyone always wondered why you didn't
put your amazing talent towards a novel.

I have wondered so many times why I felt such
intense passion to write this story — maybe it's been
you guiding me this whole time and I'm just now
figuring it out.

Table of Contents

⊷ Advice from a Manatee™ ⊷

Breathe deep

Glide through your day

Have a gentle spirit

Enjoy time alone

Eat plenty of greens

Keep your whiskers clean

Live large!

Chapter One

"STRIKE ONE," the ump yelled.

"STRIKE TWO," the ump yelled.

"STRIKE THREE!" the ump yelled, a little too enthusiastically for my liking.

"Not again," I mumbled to myself as I turned and walked back to the dugout with my bat dragging behind me, thoroughly disappointed with my performance. For the third time today, I hadn't even attempted to swing the bat.

"Hey, kid! Yeah, you! Come here. I gotta ask you something!" I heard a squeaky little voice call out from where all the bat bags were hanging at the end of the dugout. I looked around to see if anyone else had heard

1

anything, but it seemed no one had. Then I heard that same squeaky little voice again say, "Hey, kid – yeah, you! Come here. I gotta ask you something!"

This time, when I looked in the direction of that squeaky little voice, I saw an odd little dark gray head peeking out from my bat bag. It had these wiry, black whiskers poking out from its thick, dark gray snout, but it was the color of its eyes that took my breath away. It wasn't just that they were the most brilliant color of blue I'd ever seen, but the way the creature was staring at me was a little unnerving. It was as if it could read my thoughts. I stood there, almost paralyzed with indecision, unable to move any closer to the creature or turn and leave, so I simply stared right back at it.

Then the creature seemed to ooze itself farther out from deep inside my bat bag, almost as if it was coming up for air. It was then I saw that it had this thick, wrinkly, dark gray neck attached to an equally thick, dark gray torso. And then, to my complete surprise, it began waving at me to come toward him with these little, dark gray flipper-like things and calling out to me.

"WHAT THE?" I screeched.

"Hey, kid, over here. This is your bag, right?" the squeaky little voice asked as he yanked off the little baseball cap that was perched on his dark gray head and started waving it around. "Come on, man. You're really gonna want to hear what I gotta tell you! It's gonna make all the difference in the game!"

"WHAT THE?" is all I seemed to be able to say. I continued to just stand there, as if my feet were glued to the dugout floor, really just wishing it would go away and leave me alone.

"Kid, is that all you've got? 'WHAT THE?'" The creature demanded to know in a tone that sounded like it was getting a little irritated with me. "I got something important to tell you about this baseball game, and you're acting like you just saw a ghost or a monster or something! What's the matter with you, huh, kid?" the squeaky little voice asked, as if it were a perfectly normal occurrence for a creature to be hanging out in someone's bat bag giving baseball advice.

"Uh, well, I guess I'm not too sure what to say!" I said, as loudly as I dared, hoping none of my teammates would see me talking to my bat bag! What exactly should I say to a weird-looking creature with a squeaky little voice, a creature who's in my bat bag demanding to talk to me about baseball?

"What are you anyway? Why are you in my bat bag, and how did you even get in there?" I asked, as I inched my way closer to the creature.

"Come on kid, quit looking at me like I'm some freaky, scary monster. I'm just a sweet, adorable, loveable manatee. You know what a manatee is, don't you?"

"Of course I know what a manatee is!" I said, feeling kind of dumb that I was acting as if I was afraid of a manatee. "Hey, wait a minute," I whispered as I leaned in closer to the creature, just in case any of my teammates were watching me. "Can anyone else see you or hear our conversation? Or am I the only one?"

"Now that's an excellent question, kid. My answer might be a little hard for you to believe or understand right now, but I'll try to explain it as simply as I can. To most people, I just look like a sweet, little stuffed manatee. You see, it's only those that truly believe in their dreams who can see me for what I really am and hear me when I talk. Are you still with me, kid, 'cause you're looking a little pale," the creature asked.

4

"Uh, sure, I guess so," I mumbled.

"OK, good! See, I'm a Mystical Guiding Manatee, and I have many, many mystical powers, but those details aren't important right now. Do you wanna hear what I gotta say or not?" the squeaky little voice demanded, sounding quite frustrated with me, again, for my reluctance to listen to him or her or whatever it was.

I turned and looked around the dugout for one of my teammates and asked him if I had just gotten hit in the head with a baseball and was bleeding profusely. My buddy said he didn't think so, but that I did look a little pale, like I'd just seen a ghost or something. Then he looked past me and asked me why I had a stuffed animal peeking out of my bat bag. I quickly replied that it was a silly gift from my best friend and cousin Kacey. I moved closer to my bat bag and shoved the creature down as far as I could, hoping it would have the good sense to leave me alone and let me wallow in my misery by myself. Even though my teammate said I hadn't gotten hit in the head, I still felt around for a lump, or maybe even some blood, hoping that he was wrong.

"Kid, snap out of it!" the creature yelled as he popped his head out of my bat bag. Again, he waved his little baseball cap around and began working himself up into quite a lather. "No, you didn't just get hit in the head with a baseball! Come on, kid. This is just ME trying to help YOU!"

"Holy cow. What are you talking about?" I yelled back, completely forgetting, and at this point not really caring, how strange I probably looked yelling at my bat bag that had a stuffed manatee peeking out of it. "Help me with what? What kind of squishy, squeaky little creature are you anyway?"

"First off, let's get this clear. I ain't no 'creature.' I already told you, I'm a manatee — an extremely spectacular manatee, so please don't ever call me a creature again, OK? Second, we ain't got time for all these silly questions! Kid, I'm gonna get right to the point. WHY AIN'T YOU SWINGING YOUR BAT?"

"Excuse me? What the heck are you talking about? I'll have you know, I'm practically the best hitter on the team . . . well, maybe not the best, but certainly not the worst hitter. Not that I need to explain myself to you, but I am not swinging my bat 'cause this pitcher stinks. It isn't my fault he's a terrible pitcher. If he were a better pitcher, I'd be hitting the snot out of the ball."

"Oh, I get it. So now it's the pitcher's fault that you can't swing your bat! So you're saying if he were a better pitcher, then you'd be a better hitter, right?" The squeaky little manatee creature rolled his eyes and slapped me on the arm with his teeny baseball cap.

"Exactly," I exclaimed.

"Sorry, kid. I ain't buying that. It sounds more like a case of *victim-itis* if you ask me!"

"*Victim* . . . what? Dude, you aren't making any sense. You asked me why I wasn't swinging my bat, and I told you, so what's the problem?"

"No, all I heard was an excuse for why you weren't swinging your bat. You didn't give me a reason why you weren't swinging your bat. See, kid, there's a huge difference between the two. As I see it, there are two kinds of people: *victims* and *victors*. Some people like being the *victim* 'cause then it means they don't have to take responsibility for their actions. See, it's always someone else's fault; but a *victor* is someone who overcomes difficult situations and defeats the opponent.

You, young man, are acting like a *victim*, and that's a scaredy-cat way of handling things if you ask me!" the squeaky little manatee creature said, as he placed his flipper-like things on his hips and stared at me with his big blue puppy-dog eyes.

"What . . . I'm not scared! And I'm no scaredy-cat! I told you he's not throwing me any good pitches, and that umpire is just as bad; he can't tell the difference between a ball and a strike. So, like I said, it isn't my fault!"

"Oh, so now it's the umpire's fault as well. Now I get it. The pitcher's a bad pitcher, and the umpire's a bad umpire, so you're just gonna stand there. You're just gonna blame everybody else! Hey, kid, STOP LOOKING FOR SOMEBODY ELSE TO BLAME! Did you know you're putting a lot of time and energy toward blaming everybody else? How about using some of that time and energy to improve yourself? Kid, I know that you know what you need to do, but for whatever reason, you can't, or won't, let yourself do it. Kid, it's quite simple: *when you believe in your heart that you are ready and capable, then, and only then, will good things start to happen!*"

"Wait a minute! This is getting way, way too weird and starting to get a little creepy!" I said, as I backed up and sat down hard on the bench. My patience with this manatee creature was wearing thin. I was hot and sweaty from playing baseball all day. My hair was soaked with sweat, my white uniform pants were anything but white, and my cleats were too tight. "Come on, man. Give me a break. You can't really think I'm gonna believe all that mumbo-jumbo stuff, do ya? Why should I believe you? I don't even know who you are or where you're from."

"Kid, you're right. Please excuse my bad manners. How rude of me! The name's Maynard, Maynard the Mystical Guiding Manatee. YOUR Mystical Guiding Manatee. See, look here: it's on my beautiful yellow cape! Isn't this an awesome cape? I think it's the most beautiful color of yellow in the whole world. Yellow is absolutely my favorite color, and I especially love this color yellow 'cause it's not too mustardy, and it's not too orangey. It's just the perfect color yellow, ya know? Kinda like a beautiful sunflower!"

"OK, so now I know your name's Maynard, Maynard the Mystical Guiding Manatee, who wears a cool yellow cape! But the real question is why do you even care if I swing my bat? You're a manatee, remember? You're not a baseball player, you're not a coach, you're not a major league scout. You live in the water. You eat sea grass and float around all day. What the heck could you possibly know about baseball? And it seems like all you want to do is talk about your cool, yellow cape. So far you haven't explained why I should start swinging my bat."

"Kid, are you kidding me? Didn't you just hear me explain to you that you have the choice to be a *victim* or a *victor?* I feel like you are starting to make some questionable choices, choices that are going to cause you a lifetime of problems if you don't reevaluate, right now, what kind of person you want to be. I told you: I'm a Mystical Guiding Manatee, YOUR Mystical Guiding Manatee, and I have many, many mystical powers. I love, love, love the game of baseball, and I hate to see such a talented young person that has so much potential struggle so unnecessarily. Kid, this ain't entirely about swinging your bat, goofball. It's about what's in your heart and what kind of person you want to be, a victim or a victor. Do ya get it? Hey, wait a minute. Your name's Jake, right?" the creature asked, a little hesitantly.

"Yeah, it's Jake, but how did you know that? How could you possibly know that? I think I'm getting a lump where that baseball hit me in the head. Can you see it?" I asked him as I bent over for him to get a closer look.

"Kid, you didn't get hit in the head with a baseball! Gosh, how many times do I gotta tell you that? But now that I think about it, this is kind of strange. They said you were ready to have a Mystical Guiding Manatee. It seems I must have the wrong kid. Oh no! Oh no! Oh boy, I'm gonna be in some kinda trouble! This is my very first assignment, and now I've blown it! I told King Moo Moo and Queen Mee Mee that I was more than ready and now this! I begged them to let me have this assignment. I absolutely love baseball, and now . . . oh no, this is not good! Not good at all!"

I watched as Maynard's big blue puppy-dog eyes began to fill with tears; his chin sank into his chest, his shoulders slumped, and he let his little baseball cap fall to the ground.

Oh no, I thought. He's not handling this well! Holy cats, I think he's crying! Come on, Jake. Can't you think of something to say that might make him feel a little better?

"Maynard, I'm sorry that I wasn't the right kid, 'cause you're probably not that bad of a manatee to have around! I'm sure they'll forgive you! You know, since this is your first assignment, right? Maynard, is there anything I can do or anyone I can call to help you figure this out? Think, Maynard, think. Please stop crying, and just think about how to fix this!"

"Maybe I just landed in the wrong bat bag," Maynard said. "Yeah, that's it! If I can just find the right bat bag real quick, then maybe no one will even notice. Gosh, I don't know how this could've happened. Jake, if you'll just excuse me and please accept my apology, I'm very sorry for bothering you. But don't worry; I'll be gone when you get back from your next turn at bat. And if you could just do me a teeny-weeny little favor and keep this little mishap on the down low, that would be so awesome! Hmm. Jake, I just can't believe this has happened! Maybe, just maybe, it wasn't me who made a mistake? Maybe King Moo

Moo or Queen Mee Mee made the mistake? No, that's just not possible. That would be so unlike them. Well, maybe. I don't know . . .I guess mistakes can happen! Jake, I guess they thought you were one of the ones who, you know, cared about the game."

"Hey, what are you talking about? I love baseball, way more than you'll ever know. You may not know this, but I'm gonna play for the Los Angeles Angels one day, so there! And furthermore, I'm not a victim, and I am no scaredy-cat! I work really hard to be a good hitter, harder than most guys; it's just so embarrassing and frustrating to know I can hit the ball — and pretty good, too. And then, when I need to, I can't seem to hit the ball at all."

"Oh, Jake, now I'm beginning to understand. I don't think anyone has made a mistake! I get it. You're the right kid! I'm sure you're the right kid! Jake, that's the point I was trying to make! That's exactly my point, kid! '*When you believe in yourself completely, and I mean completely believe, then, and only then, will you be able to do whatever it is that you want to do.*' I promise! But you gotta believe it in your gut every minute of every day.

"You Jake, are an amazing baseball player. But today, even if they were throwing watermelons, you still wouldn't be able to hit one, and that's a fact! I guess you gotta make a choice, kid. Are you gonna continue to be a *victim* like you've been doing all day, or are you gonna run out there and take charge of your situation and be a *victor*? I'm telling ya kid, when you realize that it's all within your control, that '*your body follows your brain,*' then, and only then, will you be successful. Jake, did you hear me? 'Cause you really gotta hear this: '*your body follows your brain.*' Tell your body what you want it to do, and it *will follow*!"

"Maynard, this is almost too weird to say out loud, but for some strange reason, you're starting to make some sense. Hmm, '*my body follows my brain*'! Well, OK, Maynard, I'm gonna give it a try, and I'll let you know how it goes."

"Kid, ya can't just give it a try. Ya gotta believe it in your gut, every minute of every day! Ya just gotta decide that you can, and you will succeed. And kid, you won't have to tell me how you did, 'cause I've been watching you all day. Don't you worry – I'll know how it goes."

"Jake! Jake, are you planning to stand there all day talking to your bat bag, or would you like to go hit?" Coach yelled.

"Sorry, Coach. I'm coming!"

"STRIKE ONE," the ump yelled.

"STRIKE TWO," the ump yelled again.

"Time," I called to the ump. Come on, Jake. Not again! I took a step back and went through my routine. I adjusted my right glove, then my left glove, took a practice swing; and then took a deep breath. What was it that squeaky little manatee creature said? *'My body follows my brain. My body follows my brain'!* OK, body, let's smack the snot out of that watermelon and sail it over the fence!

"OK Ump, I'm ready."

SMACK! No way, no way. I just hit my first home run! I kept saying no way over and over in my head. Keep running, man. Keep running. First base, second base, third base, no way, home plate!

"HOLY CATS, WE JUST WON THE GAME," I started screaming. This time it was gonna be me on the bottom of the dog pile, but it was just where I wanted to be.

"JAKE, JAKE, WE WON! WE WON!" Everyone was yelling and clapping and jumping around.

"Settle down a minute guys," our coach said. "Listen here, I'm proud you didn't give up on yourselves. You worked hard all the way to the end of the game! Nicely done boys! Now, get this dugout cleaned up and go home!"

Chapter Two

"Hey, Jake, are you almost done in there?" My cousin Kacey asked, in her usual cheerful way, as she stood at the end of the dugout.

"Hang on. Let me get my cleats off, and I'll be right out," I said.

"OK! My mom is on her way to pick me up. I'll meet you at the bleachers."

"Kacey, did you get my big hit on video?" I asked, as I made my way to the bleachers where Kacey was sitting. "I sure hope so, 'cause I can't wait for Grandma to see my very first home run. You know she's gonna go crazy!"

"Come on, Jake. Of course, I got it on video. What do ya think, I'm some kinda 'ham and egger'? I'm practically a world-class videographer," Kacey teased as she was repacking her backpack that held her precious camera and video equipment.

She's a naturally gifted photographer, but her real passion is making short movies. Somehow she always ropes me into 'starring' in her projects; sometimes I pretend that I don't like it, but it's OK I guess. She comes up with some fun stuff for us to do, and we usually end up having a pretty good time.

"I don't know about world-class, but hey if you say so. I will admit you're one heck of a softball player. It was so exciting that you threw your very first no-hitter yesterday. A lot of pitchers never even come close to throwing a no-hitter, and you made it look easy. Impressive Kacey, very impressive."

"Well, I don't know about easy, but thank you for the compliment, Jake! That means a lot coming from you 'cause there's nobody that works harder at the game than you do."

"Kacey, I'm so glad you came to the game today and got my very first home run on film. Now I have actual proof that it really happened. I was starting to worry that I was going to have another terrible day at the plate. I can't wait to show Grandma my big hit."

"Yeah, she's gonna go crazy! I sure do miss her," Kacey said.

"Me too. We're lucky; she's probably the best grandma in the whole world! I sure wish we lived closer to her," I said. "My mom told me that she and your mom are planning a big family get-together at her farm this summer."

"Yeah, I heard that too," Kacey said. "That's gonna be awesome! Remember last summer when we slept out in our Top-Secret-Hideaway in Grandma's barn almost every night? The best part of the whole day was when Grandma would sneak out to our Top-Secret-Hideaway with warm chocolate chip cookies and bottles of Coke, and we would all sit around, and she would tell us those crazy stories about those magical animals that would make us laugh until our bellies ached!"

"Yeah, that was so cool," I said. "Remember that time when Grandma made us laugh so hard that Coke came out of your nose?"

"Yeah, that was pretty gross. Do you remember how hard that made Grandma laugh? But that didn't even slow her down. She just kept right on telling us those crazy stories."

"Do you remember what kind of animal it was that Grandma was always talking about in her stories?" I asked, hesitantly.

"Uh, well, maybe . . . wasn't it some kinda fish or sea creature or something like that?" Kacey said, as she struggled to remember.

"Was it a manatee?" I just kinda blurted out.

"That's right. It was a manatee. I think it lived on an island that had a weird name, like Kwallapeepee. Hey, remember when our dads snuck up the ladder and scared the daylights out of us that one night?"

"Holy cats, what if those stories were real?" I mumbled to myself, completely forgetting that Kacey was sitting there talking to me.

"Jake? Hey, are you even listening to me?" Kacey asked as she shook my arm.

"Yeah, of course, I am. You're right; our dads got us pretty good! They were so proud of themselves; they laughed about that the rest of the summer! I'm still not sure who screamed louder, you or me."

"I don't know either, Jake, but it was loud enough that our moms came running out of the house in their pajamas wondering what all the commotion was about. And then Grandma came running out carrying her broom and yelling our names. She was so scared that we were being attacked by a bear or something."

"Oh my gosh, Kacey, remember she had those funny-looking pink curlers sticking out all over her head and how her infamous pink, fuzzy slippers got all muddy from running around in the dark."

"Jake, it makes me laugh just thinking about it. Gosh, I don't think she's completely forgiven our dads for scaring her so badly or ruining her infamous pink, fuzzy slippers!"

"Well, you know our grandmother when it comes to the two of us; she's pretty protective. That sure was an amazing summer, wasn't it?"

"Whether you think you can or you think you can't you're right"

- Henry Ford -

Chapter Three

*J*ake, your mom called and told me you hit your first home run today," my aunt Bee yelled from her car. "Congratulations, buddy. I'm so happy for you! Have you seen Kacey? She called and told me she was ready to go."

"I'm right here, Mom!" Kacey yelled as she jumped off the bleachers and heaved her backpack onto her back. It weighed practically as much as she did, but that never seemed to slow her down. She readjusted her favorite vintage Angels hat, pulled her long, blond ponytail through the hole at the back of the cap, and headed to the car.

Even though Kacey was two months younger than me, she was about an inch taller. This freaked me out, but Mom kept telling me not to worry because girls always grow much faster than boys. She said I would catch up one day. Gosh, I sure hope so.

"Hi, honey," I heard Aunt Bee say. "Let's go. Dinner's ready, and your dad's starving!"

"See ya, Jake. Nice hit," Kacey said, as she was getting in the car.

"Thanks again for coming to the field today!" I yelled back. "Actually, Kacey?"

"Yeah Jake, what's up?" she asked as she stopped to make sure I was OK. She always seems to know when something is bothering me. Sometimes we are more like twins than cousins.

I was desperate to talk with her about Maynard and everything that had just happened, but I quickly changed my mind, realizing this was not the time or place to have this conversation.

"Uh, nothing. It's nothing! Really." I tried to reassure her, even though I was dying to tell her everything.

"Are you sure?"

"Yep, I'm sure. Thanks again for coming to my game."

"OK then. Call me later if you want to. I'll be up late. I've got a ton of homework. I can't believe how much more homework there is now that we're in sixth grade; sometimes I can barely keep up," Kacey said, waving as she and my aunt drove away.

"OK, thanks. See ya tomorrow at school," I mumbled as I walked back to the dugout. Hmm. I wonder if I should have told Kacey about Maynard. Nah, it's probably best I didn't say anything. I'm pretty sure I just imagined the whole thing anyway. But then I couldn't help but wonder if Maynard saw my big hit. Come on, Jake. Just go back to the dugout, get your stuff, and go home! Your parents are waiting for you. Pull yourself together. Don't you feel silly standing here wondering if a squeaky little talking manatee saw your big hit? Enough of this nonsense already! OK, I'll just take one little quick peek to see if he's in my bat bag, and if he is, I'll ask him if he saw my hit. And if he's not, then it'll prove, uh, I don't know what it

will prove. OK, here goes nothing, I thought to myself as I opened my bat bag and said, "Maynard? Hey,
Maynard? Did you see my. . . . "

Of course he wasn't in there; he's probably moved
on to his next assignment. Well, at least now I know I
can hit the snot out of the ball.

I dragged my stuff out of the dugout and back to the
locker room. I needed to change and get my books,
but I couldn't help wondering where that silly little manatee creature was and why he didn't stick
around and congratulate me on my big hit. I would've
thought that after he made all that hoopla about me
not swinging my bat and not believing in myself that
he would at least stay to see if his little pep talked
worked. Oh well, it's probably best he's gone; it
would've been awkward having him around all the
time anyway.

"Jake, are you almost ready to go?" my coach asked.
"It's getting late, and I want to kill the lights on the
field and get things locked up. I'm sure your parents
are eager to congratulate you on your big hit today."

Hey, maybe you can even talk them into a celebratory dinner. Nice job out there! I am proud of you for not quitting on yourself, even though you were having such a hard time at the plate!"

"Thanks, Coach! I'll see you tomorrow," I said as I gathered up the last of my stuff and shoved it into my backpack, realizing that I was, again, the last one to leave the locker room.

"Hey, buddy," my dad said from his usual spot on the bench right outside the locker room door. "Gosh, do you always have to be the last one out of the locker room, son? Your mom's already in the car. Let's go! Nice hit, buddy! I was sure proud of you that you were able to correct things there at the end, 'cause you were sure looking a little stinky earlier in the game! Not in the field, of course, but you were sure struggling at the plate."

"Hey, Jake," my mom said as my dad and I got in the car. "Nice hit, very nicely done! It almost seemed like you had some divine intervention out there."

"Mom, Dad, honestly, I felt like I did have some divine intervention out there. Do you believe that's possible? I mean, I felt like I had someone talking to me and helping me correct some things, and then POW, I go and hit a home run. Is that weird?"

"Well, Jake, I guess it's only weird if you believe it's weird," Mom said. "If the message worked, then isn't that all that matters?"

"Yeah, I guess you're right. Hey, Mom, when you were a little girl, did Grandma ever tell you any stories about manatees that lived on some island?"

"Yeah, I remember her telling me a few stories about manatees, but I thought they were a little silly. As I recall, there were these manatees with some kind of magical powers that lived on this island with a strange name and the manatees wore these really cool capes, but I don't remember much else. All I wanted to hear about were horses, so we read lots and lots of books about horses. Why do you ask?"

"Oh, no real reason," I said. "Kacey and I were just talking after the game and laughing about Grandma and all her crazy stories and how much fun we have with her in our Top-Secret-Hideaway. I can't wait until this summer when we go back out there. I miss her a lot."

"I know you do, buddy," Mom said, "that's why Aunt Bee and I have planned for you and Kacey to spend a little extra time out there without any of the parents around."

"Really, Mom? That's awesome! You and Aunt Bee are the best!" I said. It's gonna be the most amazing summer ever, I thought to myself.

"Courage doesn't mean you don't get afraid . . . courage means you don't let fear stop you"

- Bethany Hamilton -

Chapter Four

"Mom, Dad, thanks for taking me out to dinner. I'm gonna go take a bath, but first I think I'll call Grandma and tell her about my big hit, OK?"

"Of course, Jake! You know she loves to hear from you," Mom said as she was petting her precious cat, Bunny. Honestly, her cat freaks me out. And who names a cat Bunny anyway? She likes to sneak into my room and burrow herself under the pile of dirty clothes on my floor or under the covers on my bed and then jump out at me and scare me half to death. Of course, I yell at her for scaring me and then my mom yells at me for yelling at the cat. Why did we have to get a cat anyway, especially one named Bunny? Why couldn't we just get a cool dog, like a beagle. I love beagles.

"OK, Mom, I'll be in my bedroom."

~

"Hey, Grandma," I said as I settled myself on my bed, anxious to tell her all about my big hit.

"Hello, honey. How are you? I'm so glad you called! I've had this peculiar feeling about you all day. So tell me, what's been going on?" Grandma said. She has this way of making me feel like no matter what she's doing, it's never more important than talking with me.

"Oh my gosh, Grandma, I hit my very, very first home run today! It was so awesome, and it was the winning hit. Can you believe it?"

"Oh, Jake, honey of course I can believe it. That's so wonderful! I'll bet you were yelling and jumping all over the place! Tell me all about it honey, but first, tell me, did Kacey get it on film?"

"Of course she did, Grandma. You know Kacey and her cameras; she's always filming something. She's gonna send it to you. I sure hope she posts it on her

YouTube channel so maybe I'll get discovered by the Los Angeles Angels! Grandma, but there's something else I need to talk to you about," I whispered, as I got up to close my bedroom door. "I don't have a lot of time to talk right now, and I don't want Mom and Dad to overhear me, so I'll have to give you the short version."

"OK honey, I understand," Grandma said. "Just tell me as much as you can."

"Well, I was having the most horrible day at the plate. I struck out three times, and the worst part is that I wasn't even swinging the bat. I had lost all my confidence and was having a miserable day. After my third ugly strikeout, I dragged myself back to the dugout and was feeling completely worthless as a hitter. I hated that I was letting my team down. I was so frustrated with myself because I've spent so many hours in the batting cage working on my hitting and it wasn't helping me at all. I was just standing in the dugout, beating myself up, when I heard this squeaky little voice call out to me from the end of the dugout where all of the bat bags were hanging. I looked down the row of bat bags, and I saw this creature with an odd little dark-gray head peeking out from my bat bag. Then the squeaky little creature said he had something important to tell me about the game and that I really needed to come closer and listen to him. At first I tried to ignore him, hoping he would just go away and leave me alone. But he was so adamant that he could help me if I would just take his advice, so I scooched a little closer. He then proceeded to tell me that he's a very spectacular manatee by the name of Maynard, 'Maynard the Mystical Guiding Manatee.' Oh yeah, and he was wearing a really cool cape! Grandma, can you believe this? And then it gets even weirder. I actually took his advice — I still don't even know why — and, as it turns out, he's the reason I hit a home run. Can you believe that?"

"Well, Jake, yes, I can believe it, but go on. Tell me more!"

"What did you just say?" I shrieked.

"Never mind right now, Jake, we don't have much time. Please just continue with your story," Grandma pleaded.

"Well, he starts off by asking me why I wasn't swinging my bat, and then the next thing I know, he starts lecturing me, telling me I'm acting like a victim and a scaredy-cat. Grandma, at this point I just wanted to zip up my bat bag and toss it out of the dugout! But he quickly tells me that all I gotta do is believe that *my body follows my brain!* Then he says, 'Jake, it's very, very simple, tell your body what you want it to do, believe in yourself, and then good things will happen!' The next thing I know, my coach is yelling at me that I'm on deck. So, I decided, what the heck I can't possibly hit any worse than I have been, so I took Maynard's advice and told myself to just hit the snot out of the ball, and I did. And we won the game. Can you believe it? Grandma, is there something wrong with me? Is it really possible that there was a Mystical Guiding Manatee in my bat bag, giving me advice on how to hit a baseball? Do you think I need to go to the doctor or something?"

"Honey, there's nothing wrong with you, I promise," Grandma said. "Jake, I know this is going to be hard for you to understand right now, but you've been chosen to receive an amazing gift! I had a feeling that since it didn't happen to your mother or your Aunt Bee that it would happen to either you or Kacey. Oh, sweetheart, I am so happy for you! I know this seems very strange right now, but please, just trust me. This is going to be the most amazing thing that has ever happened to you. Jake, you must find the courage to embrace this. Remember what I've always told you and Kacey?"

"Yeah, yeah, Grandma, I know, '*Courage doesn't mean you don't get afraid . . . courage means you don't let fear stop you*' but what's that got to do with any of this?"

"Jake, it's got everything to do with this! Please promise me that you will keep your heart open and you won't let fear take hold. You will be just fine, I promise. Trust me when I say, wherever your travels take you, when you're on Maynard's back, your safety is never in question, and no harm will ever come your way. Now, do you need me to come out and help?"

"Help? Help with what? What do you mean, 'wherever your travels take you'? He's just a little stuffed animal! How am I going to travel on the back of a stuffed animal? And where exactly is he gonna take me? Grandma, this is nuts! This is just crazy,

crazy talk!" I ranted. I think I was even starting to sound a little hysterical and then it hit me.

"Ooooh," I laughed as it dawned on me. "Now I get it. You and Kacey are playing a joke on me, right? I gotta admit, I fell for it. I don't know how you guys pulled this off, but that's OK, have a good laugh at my expense. I tip my hat to you both; this was a good one. But don't worry, I'll get even. It might take me awhile to top this one but trust me, I'll find a way. Grandma, you can call Kacey and tell her the gig's up, the joke's over. I figured it out. I'm not mad but I will get even."

"Jake, honey, are you quite done?" Grandma asked without a hint of laughter in her voice. "Kacey and I are not playing a trick on you, and this is not a joke. I give you my word. Something very special is happening to you, and it will all make sense, all in good time. Please do not be frightened. I promise you this will be the most magical time of your life."

"Well, OK then," I said. "I know how protective you are of me and Kacey, so if you say it'll be OK, I'll trust you. I will try my hardest not to be frightened. I'm really glad I called you, and I love you very much. Thank you for being such a special grandma. I haven't seen Maynard since the ball field, but I'll call you if or when I see him again."

"Oh Jake, you will see him again. I promise you; you're going to see him again! Is his cape yellow, by chance?"

"Grandma, now you are really starting to freak me out! How could you know his cape was yellow?" I said as I jumped off my bed and started pacing back and forth in my room, trying not to trip over all the dirty clothes that were starting to pile up.

"Oh Jake, there is so much to tell you, but now is definitely not the right time. I promise you one day I will tell you the entire story, from beginning to end. Honey, please call me when you see Maynard again, and I'll come out to give you the cover you'll need."

"OK, I'll call you, even though I really don't understand what you're talking about."

"Jake, we really shouldn't talk about this anymore over the phone. Honey, I love you, and I am so happy for you! Give Maynard a big hug for me and tell him Vicki-Lou sends her love!"

"WHAT?" I cried out as I flung myself across my bed, landing squarely on top of Bunny, who had burrowed herself under my covers again. She let out a piercing yowl and flew off the bed. Heaven help me if I squished Bunny and hurt her; not even Maynard the Mystical Guiding Manatee would be able to help me out of that mess.

"Jake, honey, no more questions. It's too risky. Not a word to your mom and dad, or anyone for that matter. But don't forget what I have always told you: *'Courage doesn't mean you don't get afraid . . . courage means you don't let fear stop you.'* Bye for now, honey!" And with a click on the other end of the line, she was gone.

Holy cats, I thought to myself. What the heck is going on? This has been such a weird day, and it just got even weirder.

Chapter Five

"Hey, kid, nice hit today!" I heard that same squeaky little voice announce from somewhere in the bathroom.

"WHAT THE? Come on, man. Can't a guy even have a little privacy in the tub?" I grumbled as Maynard jumped up on the side of the tub, with a silly grin on his face and his baseball cap perched on his head.

"There you go again with the 'WHAT THE's. Is that all you've ever got to say, huh? Hey, kid, maybe you could try something like, 'Oh, hello there, Maynard, my Mystical Guiding Manatee. It's so wonderful to see you again!' Or you might say something like, 'Gee, Maynard, your cape is sure looking magnificent tonight!'" he said as he spun around making his cape fly out behind him. "But no, all you can say is 'WHAT THE?' Jake, if you can't be nicer to me, then maybe, just maybe, I should come back later when you're not such a grouchy bear!" he said as he turned to jump off the side of the tub.

"Maynard, what are you talking about? I'm not a grouchy bear! It's just that you keep appearing and disappearing; it's just kinda freaky, that's all! And I just thought that, you know, maybe you were gonna stick around and watch me hit!" I said feeling a little embarrassed having admitted this to him.

"Hey, what do ya mean? I saw your big hit! Kid, I wasn't gonna miss that for anything in the world! You hit that big, fat watermelon all the way over the fence, just like you said you were gonna do." He raised his flipper to his forehead and pretended to watch it fly out of sight. "Don't think for one minute that just 'cause you didn't see me that I didn't see you!"

"Really, you saw it? What'd ya think? Pretty awesome, huh?"

"Jake, I'm gonna say it again and again and again until you start believing it! We all knew that once you started to believe in yourself, amazing things were gonna happen!"

"We? Who do you mean by we?" I asked as I slid down farther into the tub, grateful I still had so many bubbles left in my bath.

"King Moo Moo, Queen Mee Mee, and ME, of course!" Maynard said as he puffed up his little gray chest and attempted to flex his not-so-impressive biceps.

"And what exactly is a King Moo Moo and a Queen Mee Mee?" I asked, not too sure I really wanted to hear the answer.

"They are the king and queen of the Mystical Guiding Manatees of The Lagoon, of course!" Maynard declared, walking back and forth on the edge of the tub, waving his little baseball cap around. He seems to do that when he gets excited.

"Oh, my gosh, Maynard. Just when I thought this day couldn't get any weirder, you show up again and start telling me about kings and queens! Why are you here? What do you want from me? What could you possibly want from me?" I asked him, probably a little louder than I should have, all the while hoping that Maynard had exceptionally good balance and didn't end up slipping and falling into the tub with me.

"Jake, I really do understand that you're having a little trouble understanding all of this, but I promise you it will get less and less weird as soon as I tell you all about me and where I'm from! Oh, by the way, I have some amazing news! You can rest assured, 'cause I triple checked. They didn't send me to the wrong kid! In fact, you've been on their radar for quite a while now. We – the king, the queen, and I – got it all straightened out; I'm definitely assigned to be YOUR Mystical Guiding Manatee! Jake, it's you and me, kid, all the way!"

"You and me all the way where, exactly?" I couldn't help but ask.

"Jake? Jake, honey, who are you talking to?" my mom asked through the bathroom door.

"Uh, no one really, Mom. Just singing a silly little song that I just made up. I guess I just got a little carried away!"

"Are you sure you would call that singing? It sure didn't sound like singing to me. Are you almost done in there? It's getting late."

"Yes, ma'am, I'm almost done." I said. I waited to hear her shut my bedroom door and then turned to Maynard and said, "We've gotta be way more careful. The last thing I need is for my mom to start asking me a billion questions. We gotta just whisper, OK?"

"No problem! Hey, when you're ready and it's safe for us to talk, I'll tell you all about me, where I'm from, and why I'm here, but I can't have you freaking out and getting your panties all twisted in a knot, OK?"

"Uh, just for the record, I don't go around getting my panties all twisted up in knots. Go ahead, get started. I'm as ready as I'm ever gonna be, so let's have it, and I promise, no freaking out!"

Maynard took a minute and made himself a comfy seat on the side of the tub with his cool cape. "Well, as you know my name is Maynard, Maynard the Mystical Guiding Manatee. Cool name, huh? It's almost as cool as my cape! And, as I've stated, I'm a manatee. I'm from a mystical island somewhere in the South Pacific called Kahwallawallapoopoo. It's pronounced

KAH-WALLA-WALLA-POO-POO – pretty cool name, huh? Jake, it's the most beautiful island on the planet!

"I live on the Island of Kahwallawallapoopoo with my family and friends in a mystical lagoon. Our lagoon is on one side of Kahwallawallapoopoo; the other side of Kahwallawallapoopoo is a lush tropical forest. The Lagoon has been home to the Mystical Guiding Manatees for centuries because we have one of the world's most vibrant coral reefs on the planet that protects us from the harsh weather conditions that can occur in the South Pacific Ocean. Not to mention, the coral reef also helps protect us from surprise visits from uninvited guests.

"The other side of the island is home to the WallaPoo people and is equally as beautiful as The Lagoon, but in a much different way. It's densely populated with huge trees that are thousands of years old, hundreds of species of beautiful flowers and green leafy plants of all sizes and shapes, some creepy crawly bugs, and some funny looking slimy creatures as well. In one section of the forest, the branches have grown together and weaved a massive shelf-like structure.

The WallaPoo people have built their entire village on this shelf-like structure. It protects them from the flooding that happens every year during our rainy season and also helps keep some of the creepy bugs and funny looking slimy creatures that live on the flowers and plants from invading their houses.

"But Jake, the most remarkable aspect of our entire island is the water in The Lagoon. Its mystical properties are essential to the well-being of all the creatures that thrive on our little island. It's the most brilliant color of blue-green you've ever seen. It's so spectacular that it even sparkles at night. You'll see what I mean as soon as we get there. I promise you're gonna love it."

"Wait just a minute! Hold on!" I sat up so quickly that I splashed bath water all over Maynard and his cool cape, nearly knocking him off the side of the tub. "What did you just say? I'm going to The Lagoon? And how exactly will I be getting there, Maynard?" I blurted out completely forgetting to whisper.

"Jake, you promised you wouldn't freak out, so please just let me finish! I'm trying to help you understand, but if you keep interrupting me —"

"OK, OK," I said. "I'm listening! But this is getting weirder than the conversation I just had with my grandmother."

Maynard began to wring out his cool cape and his little baseball cap and situated himself again. "As I was saying, the water in our lagoon is not only beautiful, but it has many miraculous powers."

"Powers, really? Like what kind of powers?" I blurted out. "Can I make a wish and the magical water will grant me whatever I want, like a new bat or a fancy new glove or a really cool new bike? Hey, maybe the magical water can make it so every time I'm up to bat I'll hit a home run? Maynard, this is gonna be so totally cool!"

This seemed to be the last straw for Maynard. He jumped up from his cool cape seat, threw his flippers in the air and said, "Come on, Jake. I said mystical not magical! I'm not like a genie in a bottle here to grant you three wishes. If that's what you think this is all about then I'm just gonna go home. I'm gonna tell my mom and dad that they made a big mistake — you're not the kid they thought you were, and boy is Vicki-Lou gonna be disappointed in you when she hears that your Mystical Guiding Manatee quit before you even went on your first adventure," Maynard announced. He threw his little cap on the floor, jumped up on the counter, put both of his little flippers on his hips and stared down at me with the saddest look on his face.

Oh no. I think I got a little carried away. From the look on Maynard's face, I knew I'd really hurt his feelings. He has that same look my mom gives me when I've said or done something really hurtful or unkind to someone and she tells me how 'disappointed' she is in me. To me that's the worst; I would rather she just get mad and send me to my room. I felt like a real schmuck.

"Maynard, I'm sorry. I didn't mean to make fun of you or your mystical island. I just got a little carried away. Will you please accept my apology? I was just being a schmuck. I know you're not a genie from a bottle; you're way too cool to live in a bottle! Will you please finish telling me about Kahwallawallapoopoo?" I said as I leaned over and picked his little cap off the floor and set it on the side of the tub, hoping he would jump down and forgive me.

"Yeah Jake you are a schmuck! A first-class schmuck and a big meany!" Maynard said as he jumped back to the side of the tub. He picked up his little cap, slapped it on his flipper a few times, and just stood there a minute without saying a word.

"So, where was I before I was so rudely interrupted?" Maynard asked as he started pacing back and forth, waving his cap around. I guess he was trying to figure out what else he wanted to tell me about his mystical island. I was going to give him all the time he needed to collect his thoughts 'cause I knew I'd almost blown it by making fun of him, and I was starting to kind of like having him around.

And then Maynard stopped dead in his tracks. He was no longer waving his cap around or pacing back and forth. He just stood there with his eyes closed, flippers hanging limp, seemingly deep in thought. I had absolutely no idea what to say or do, so I just waited for him to collect his thoughts. And then as quickly as he had stopped, his head bolted upright, his eyes flew open, and he announced, "Jake, I'm gonna take the high-road. I'm a Mystical Guiding Manatee, and it's my responsibility to guide. I feel I have let you down by not fully explaining to you the difference between a mystical manatee and a magical manatee. So, if you would, please accept my apology for assuming that you understood something that you had no way of understanding and allow me to provide you with a brief explanation of the differences between mystical and magical."

"Uh, sure Maynard, that would be great," was all I could think of to say, as this sudden turn of events was kind of strange. But hey, everything about this day has been strange, so why should this be any different!

"Hmm, where to start," Maynard mumbled as he busied himself making another cool cape seat. Once he was all settled in, he looked up at me and started explaining.

"Mystical and magical — two words that seem to be very similar and sometimes can be used to describe the same thing or event, except when you are describing the manatees of The Lagoon from the Island of Kahwallawallapoopoo. When most people think of someone or something being magical, they often associate it with witchcraft and wizardry, someone that can grant wishes and cast spells, with the intention of causing either good or evil. Oh, and they ride around on broomsticks. We cannot grant wishes or cast spells, and if I tried to ride on a broomstick I would probably really hurt myself. Therefore, the word mystical better defines the manatees of The Lagoon from the Island of Kahwallawallapoopoo. Our motivation to use our extraordinary, highly unusual, remarkable, phenomenal, and exceptional abilities is always focused on the improvement and advancement of those around us. We never, never, never use our abilities to harm or injury anyone or anything. So, Jake, have I made it completely clear to you why we refer to ourselves as 'mystical' and not 'magical'?"

"Yes, Maynard, crystal clear! Thank you for that clarification; that really helps me to understand you and your world a little better." Whew, I thought to myself, I'm so glad we got the cleared up. I don't ever want to make that mistake again."

"So, as I was saying, these extraordinary powers have made it possible for our manatee families and the WallaPoo people to thrive for thousands of years. The WallaPoo people have lived on the Island of Kahwallawallapoopoo as long as the manatees have.

Their village is remarkable! Jake, they are incredible people. Let me just say, you will feel like you've known them your whole life once you meet them. They too have a king that governs them. His name is King Peetar the Fifth; he would do anything for the WallaPoo people. In fact, he has made many significant sacrifices for them.

"The WallaPoo people are smart, hardworking, healthy, compassionate, and loving people who cherish their island and adore their king. Jake, you are going to soon realize that I am much, much more than just a sweet little talking stuffed manatee. When the conditions are right, I transform into a full-size manatee with incredible mystical powers. Once I am my HUGE, AMAZING, BIG-BAD-BUFF SELF and you are on my back, we can GO ANYWHERE you want to go, DO ANYTHING you want to do, and SEE ANYTHING you want to see."

Just as Maynard was finishing his rant, I realized he was getting pretty worked up and quite loud.

"Jake? Jake, honey, who are you talking to?" Oh my gosh, I hadn't even heard my mom open my bedroom door.

"Uh, no one, Mom! Uh, I'm still just singing away, making up these silly songs as I go! What do you think? Is my singing getting any better?"

"Well Jake, it didn't sound too much like you were singing. I am quite sure that I heard voices!"

"Come on, Mom, it's just little ol' me singing away!"

"Well, OK then. Why don't you wrap it up soon? Aren't you getting a little wrinkly? You've been in there quite a while now!"

"Well, yes. I am quite wrinkly, but at least I'm clean; I'm super, super clean!"

"That's good to know, but wrap it up, will you?"

"Will do, Mom! Maynard, we must be much quieter," I whispered. "I hate that I just lied to my mom, but if she knew I was in here talking with a manatee named Maynard, she might lose her cookies!"

"OK, Jake, I understand. But, did you just say cookies? 'Cause I really, really love cookies! Have I told you how much I love cookies? I love cookies so much . . . !"

"Maynard, shh!"

"There you go again, getting your panties all twisted in a knot. OK, OK already! We'll talk later after everyone has gone to bed. I promise to be much, much quieter! By the way, you might want to get out of that tub, 'cause you're starting to look as wrinkly as me!" He laughed as he jumped off the side of the tub and back onto the counter.

Chapter Six

"Mom, Mom I'm ready for bed," I yelled from my bedroom. "Can you come tuck me in?"

"Aw, Jakey wants his mommy to come kiss him good night. Isn't that sweet!" I heard that squeaky little voice say with a snicker from somewhere in my room.

"Maynard, where are you?" I demanded as loud as I dared.

"Jake, you're ready for bed already?" my mom asked, as she walked down the hallway. "Are you feeling OK? You never go to bed without me nagging you to turn out the light and go to sleep!"

"No Mom, I'm fine. I'm just tired; it must have

been all that singing. And don't forget about that big hit I had today!" I reminded her as she walked into my room and stood beside my bed.

"Well, OK. Are you sure you're feeling OK? You don't seem to have a fever," she said, as she pressed her hand to my forehead. Then she leaned over and kissed me on the cheek, adjusted the covers, and told me she loved me. I was sure I heard Maynard giggling from somewhere in the room.

"Mom, I'm fine! Just tired. Don't worry. Good night, Mom. I love you too!"

"Good night, honey, I love you more!" she said as she always does, turning off the light and shutting the door as she left.

"Maynard . . . Maynard . . . can you hear me? Maynard, where are you? I know you're in here somewhere."

"He-he-he . . . Jakey, I'm right here. I'm right here on the pillow next to you!" Maynard teased as he began jumping up and down on my pillow.

"Eeek! WHAT THE . . . ? Maynard, I swear, if you do that to me again, I'm gonna call your momma. Listen, you've gotta stop appearing and disappearing like that; it's really freaking me out. I never know where you are or when you're gonna show up!" I whispered loudly.

"There you go again, getting your panties all twisted in a knot. I was just having a little fun. Jake, there's one thing you'll never have to worry about, and that's me wandering too far from you. I'll always be here for you. All you need to do is call my name, and I'll come to life instantly!" Maynard said, as he jumped from the pillow to my chest.

"Maynard, shh! Remember you promised you would be much quieter! Now get off my chest and settle down! What am I gonna tell my mom if she comes back in my room demanding to know who I'm talking to, huh?"

"Hey, I know, you could tell her you were just trying to comfort poor sweet little Bunny that you almost squished to death when you were talking with Vicki-Lou!"

"Maynard, how did you know that I almost squished Bunny to death?" I said as I jumped out of bed. In my haste to get to the light switch, I nearly crashed into the wall as I tripped over the dirty clothes piling up on my floor. When I flipped on the light, both Bunny and Maynard were staring at me from my bed, their eyes as big as saucers.

"Jake, shh! I thought you promised you weren't gonna go all goofy on me. It's not important right now how I knew you almost squished poor sweet little Bunny to death," Maynard said as he scratched Bunny in her favorite spot behind her ear. "Really, it's not that big of a deal. Please, turn off the light and get back in bed. I have so much more to tell you. Listen, while I was waiting for you to give me the all clear, I had the most brilliant idea. Jake, I must say, this idea is a doozy. I think I'm gonna earn some big, fat brownie points with King Moo Moo and Queen Mee Mee for this one! Hey, have I told you that you're my very first assignment? I just want the king and queen to be proud of me!"

"Yes, Maynard, you've already told me all that. Now, what's your doozy of an idea?" I asked, as I killed the lights and jumped over my growing pile of dirty clothes, landing squarely on my bed and, thankfully, not on Bunny or Maynard.

"How about we take a super quick trip to Kahwallawallapoopoo tonight? I promise you we'll only be gone for about two hours. We'll wait until your parents are sound asleep and then we'll make a break for it! What do ya say, huh? Please, please, please, Jake, please let me take you to Kahwallawallapoopoo. I'm so anxious to introduce you to everyone. I know they are dying to meet you as well. Please, please, please say yes."

"Really, Maynard? You're kidding, right? All the way to Kahwallawallapoopoo? And back? Do all of this before I have to get up for school? Without any-one knowing I've been gone? Maynard, I promise you if my parents wake up and I'm not here, believe me — my mom will have the FBI out looking for me!"

"No problem, Jake! Easy-peasy, it'll be a piece of cake. See, what you don't know is that our time zone is a little different from your time zone. One hour of your time is about twelve hours of our time; we can get a lot done in a short amount of your time."

"Oh, OK," I said, completely confused with Maynard's math and exactly how his time zone works.

But it sounds like he understands it, so I guess that's all that matters, I thought to myself. "Well, if you're completely sure that we'll be back before my parents wake up, then I guess we could go. Why not, right? My grandmother said I would be completely safe with you, so let's go," I said, hoping this crazy manatee didn't end up getting me in a whole bunch of trouble.

"YIPPEEEE, YIPPEEEE. We're going to Kahwallawallapoopoo!" Maynard started squealing as he was bouncing up and down on my bed.

"Shh Maynard, shh! Remember, you promised!"

Maynard clapped his flippers over his mouth for a minute and then whispered, "Jake, I'm so sorry, I just get so excited about going home that I can barely contain myself. Maybe I should just break out into my happy dance instead. I know, I know, my silent happy dance. When do you think we can leave? I gotta make some arrangements. I gotta let everyone know that we're coming! Oohhh, they're gonna be so excited to meet you, Jake!"

"I'll go check and see if my parents are asleep yet. You stay right here in my room. Do not leave my room. Do you understand Maynard?" I asked, getting out of my bed and carefully making my way to the door. Before I left, I turned back to Maynard and reminded him to stay put.

"Oh, yes, Jake, I completely understand. I will try my hardest to stay right here in your bed, right next to Bunny. I promise." He raised his flipper like he was taking an oath as I quietly opened my door to leave.

As I walked down the hall toward the kitchen, I heard my bedroom door open and Maynard's squeaky little voice saying, "Jake . . . Jake! Jake, where are you?"

"Maynard, you promised!" I said as he waddled toward me.

"Uh, Jake, technically I only promised to 'try my hardest to stay in your bedroom' and, well . . ."

"Maynard, go back, right now!"

"But, Jake, I need to tell you something. I got this terrible tickle in my throat. Can you get me some water?"

"Maynard, go!"

"OK, OK, but, Jake, just one more thing. You got any cookies? I got this terrible sweet tooth and, uh, maybe a dozen or two of some oatmeal raisin cookies but without the raisins, of course. I don't know if you know this or not, but raisins, they, uh, they kinda make me *fart*!"

"Maynard, good grief. Don't you have any manners? You can't just say *fart* . . . can't you just say something like 'they give me a little gas'?"

"Well, Jake, it's way more than just a little bit of gas. It's baaaadddd! And hey, I can say *fart* when it's just you and me, but I'll tell you if my momma heard me say the *fart word*, she would —"

"Stop, Maynard, stop! It doesn't matter because we don't have any oatmeal cookies with or without raisins! Hey, I have an idea. How about if I ask my mom if she'll bake us a couple hundred dozen cookies tomorrow! I'm pretty sure she won't mind, especially when I tell her it's for this little stuffed talking manatee named Maynard, who happens to be a Mystical Guiding Manatee with a really cool cape and a terrible sweet-tooth!"

"Really, you would do that for me?" Maynard asked as he jumped up onto the counter, crashing into a box that he apparently didn't see in his haste to ask me more about finding him some cookies.

"Maynard, go!" I whispered, as I lunged for the box before it hit the floor.

"Jake, honey, is that you in the kitchen? Is there someone with you? It seems like I keep hearing you talking to someone," Mom asked me from her room.

"Sorry, Mom. I just needed some water! I've got that stupid song stuck in my head that I was singing earlier. I seem to be singing it over and over! I'm sorry, didn't mean to wake you."

"OK, Jake. Good night."

"Good night, Mom! Hey, Mom, is Dad asleep yet?"

"Almost, honey. Now please go to bed."

"Yes, ma'am!"

"Maynard," I whispered, "you've gotta stop that!" I scolded him and scooped him up with one hand, the bottle of water with the other and headed down the hall to my room. "My mom's practically convinced that I'm hiding someone from her!"

"Jake, I'm so sorry for not listening to you," Maynard said, as I placed him on the bed and gave him the bottle of water. "It's just that I got myself so excited about our trip to Kahwallawallapoopoo that I ended up with a little tickle in my throat. If I don't drink a whole bunch of water, then it will turn into a full-blown coughing fit, and believe me — you don't want that to happen. One time I started coughing so hard that it lasted for half an hour, and it was so loud that I sounded like a barking seal!"

"OK, I get it, but don't drink too much, or you're gonna need to go to the bathroom!"

"Well, now that you mention it . . ."

"No, Maynard, you're just gonna have to hold it! Hey, how exactly are we gonna get to Kahwalla-wallapoopoo? Since you've got that cool, yellow cape, are we gonna fly like Superman, or are you gonna wave a magic wand and 'poof,' we'll teleport to your magical island? What's the deal?"

"Jake, remember that I said MYSTICAL, not MAGICAL. So no, goofball, I don't have a magic wand, and even though I have a really cool cape, I can't fly like Superman. But what I can do is perhaps the coolest thing ever. See, once my sweet, adorable, little self gets wet, I transform into a full-size manatee. Kid, I'm quite impressive! I can't wait for you to see me and my HUGE, AMAZING, BIG-BAD-BUFF SELF!"

"Oh yeah, Maynard, I'll bet you're really impressive," I said, as I looked at my own skinny arms and long skinny legs, hoping that one day I'll be as big and buff as Maynard says he is. My dad keeps telling me not to worry, that all I have to do is just keep working out and eating well, and it'll happen.

"Jake, you just wait. I'm HUGE! I'm twelve hundred pounds of sheer muscle!"

"Maynard, sheer muscle? That's a little hard for me to imagine. All the manatees I've seen are huge all right, but in a blubbery, squishy, and mushy kind of way, not in a muscular, buff kind of way! But hey, maybe I'm wrong. Maybe you're different!"

"Yes, yes, you are quite wrong! I'll have you know; I'm quite impressive! I am most definitely not a mushy manatee. I am Maynard the Mystical Guiding Manatee, and I'd appreciate it if you would not forget that!"

"OK, I'm sure you are impressive all right. I'm sorry. You're right. I did forget about the mystical part. Please accept my apology! So, what's the deal? What are we gonna do? Sneak out, run to the river, jump in, wait for you to get all big and buff, and then float on into the South Pacific Ocean?"

Maynard rolled his eyes and threw his baseball cap down again and said, "No, we're not gonna run to the river, jump in, and blah, blah, blah! We're gonna go into the bathroom, then we'll get in the tub, you'll grab hold of my cape, and we will shoot down through the drain, and when we pop out, we'll be in the Pacific Ocean! Easy peasy! Then you will get the ride of your life on my back as we make our way to Kahwallawallapoopoo!"

"Holy cats, Maynard that sounds awesome! How fast can you swim?"

"Oh, about two hundred miles an hour!"

"No way!"

"Well, no. But I might be able to if there were a herd of sharks chasing me."

"Come on, Maynard. How fast can you swim?"

"Well, I can swim about sixty to eighty miles an hour, but the coolest thing about me is that I can do some pretty radical tricks!"

"Really? Like what?"

"How about if we quit talking about everything that I can do? Let's just do it!"

"All right then, let's go. I'm as ready as I'm ever gonna be!" I said, sounding a lot more confident than I felt, but hey, what's the worst thing that can happen, right? Then I remembered that Grandma said wherever my travels take me with Maynard, no harm will ever come my way.

"Jake, once we get into the tub you must follow my instructions to the letter; any variation from my instructions could cause us countless difficulties getting through the Time Warp Tunnel. Look me in the eye and tell me you will follow my instructions perfectly, without any variation or hesitation? Because if not, let me know right now, and we won't even attempt this journey," Maynard said, as he stood on my bed with both flippers on his hips, looking as somber as I have ever seen him.

"Yeah, yeah, I guess," I said, starting to feel like this was gonna be a lot more complicated than I had originally anticipated.

"Well OK then, if that's the best answer you've got, I'll take you at your word, 'cause once we start through the Time Warp Tunnel, there ain't no turning back, OK?"

"All right already, let's go!" I said, pacing back and forth in my room.

I was starting to feel a little nauseous, like the time I almost barfed on the team bus from the stench of our sweaty baseball team. We had just played two games in the hot sun. We were filthy and smelled like rotten eggs. We begged the coach to turn up the air conditioning, but he said it was broken and to just put the windows down.

"OK, OK. Don't get your panties all twisted in a knot!" Maynard said.

"This is how it's gonna happen: you're gonna climb into the tub, face the drain, and sit with your legs crossed, right over left, not left over right. Jake, it's very important that your legs are crossed right over left. Then you will gently set me in front of you about three inches from the drain hole. I will then dispense, from a very specially designed vial, eight freshly picked berries from the Yuckapouie plant, four for each of us. They contain a time-released serum that will shrink us small enough to fit through the drain and then transform us back to our original size.

"Wait just a minute! Wait one minute! What do you mean we have to eat berries from a specially designed vial? I haven't seen you with a vial or berries. Where have you been hiding all this stuff?" I asked in complete disbelief.

"In one of my pockets, of course," Maynard declared. "I've got secret pockets everywhere."

"Oh, of course you do," I mumbled. "Of course manatees have secret pockets. I should have known that."

"Not all manatees, Jake, just the mystical ones," Maynard said with a big silly grin on his face.

"So, as I was saying, once we have each eaten our four little berries from the Yuckapouie plant, we are going to have a very short amount of time to get through the drain. If the serum starts to wear off before we get through the drain then, well, I'm sure you can imagine how disastrous that will be. Are you with me so far?"

"Yep, I'm good! Right over left and four berries each. OK, let's go!" I said.

"Wait a minute, just hold your horses. There's a bit more to this process than just those two steps. Before we eat our berries, I need to let the Chief Vibrational Conch Blower at The Lagoon know that we're ready for our Vibrational Signal to be sent so that we can get sucked into the drain."

"WHAT? What the heck is a Chief Vibrational Conch Blower and how in the world is he or she or whoever going to blow into a conch shell hard enough for it to reach us here in my bathtub? Maynard, this is starting to sound really hokey," I said as I flopped down on my bed, wondering if this was really happening or if I had fallen asleep and was having one of the strangest dreams of my life.

"Well, Mr. Smarty-Farty-Pants, if you would just let me explain instead of getting all wound up, it will all make complete sense to you," Maynard demanded as he jumped up on my chest.

"Do you see this?" Maynard demanded as he whipped his cape off and held the clasp about an inch from my face. "This is way, way more than just a beautiful clasp that holds my perfectly yellow cape together: this is my very own MGS!"

"OK, I give up. What's a MGS?" I asked as I picked him up off my chest and set him down next to me. I wanted to examine the clasp that Maynard had handed me and referred to as his MGS.

"You know what a GPS is, right? Well, this is the Mystical Guiding Manatee version of a GPS. It's my 'Manatee Guidance System'! How else do you think I could successfully navigate my way around this big amazing planet all by my sweet little self?"

"You see, all Mystical Guiding Manatees have their own unique conch vibrational signal that their MGS connects to. Not only does it help us get where we need to go, but it's also how we communicate with the manatees in The Lagoon from wherever we are in the world. Oh, and the other cool thing is that it comes with this really cool MGS wristband for you," Maynard said as he started searching for the secret pocket he had put it in.

"Uh, Jake, give me just a minute, will you? It's here somewhere. I promise it's in one of these pockets. Oh heavens, why can't I find it? I know it's here somewhere because I was admiring it earlier. Don't you worry, Jake, I'll find it!" Maynard said as he started jumping up and down on the bed.

I think he was hoping that maybe it would fall out of one of his pockets, and when that didn't happen, he began frantically searching all of his pockets, again.

"Oh, here it is! I found it, yep, right where I put it, in my most secret pocket. Here you go, Jake."

"Wow, this is awesome," I said as I took the MGS band from Maynard's outstretched flipper and slipped it easily on my wrist. It was like a super cool, futuristic watch. The band was a sleek and shiny, metallic yellow, the same color yellow as Maynard's cape, of course. But it was the face of the band that made it look so high-tech. There was a deep chocolate brown screen in the shape of a triangle in the center of the band.

"Jake, so that I don't overwhelm you, I'm only going to tell you a couple of things about your MGS band right now, I'll tell you more about all of the really cool things that it can do later. First, it's completely waterproof, and second, the brown triangle is a touch screen that will give you access to tons of cool features. When you tap the screen, a capital letter 'M' will appear. Of course the 'M' will be yellow and it stands for Maynard. The most important feature of your MGS band that you need to be concerned with on this trip is the blue triangle that will light up and blink like crazy when something new is about to happen. This warning system will help you during all of our journeys, but it will come in especially handy on our first journey through the Time Warp Tunnel.

"There is also a red triangle that will flash if there is an emergency, like if we needed to get you home ASAP, but we don't need to worry about that one on this trip since we don't have a Guardian helping us."

"Gosh Maynard, this is really special, but now I feel bad that I don't have anything really cool to give to you."

"Well Jake, it's not really that kind of a gift. This is just another really cool benefit of having a Mystical Guiding Manatee. Now that you have your own MGS band, you and I will be forever synced; when you wear your MGS band, we will always be able to find each other, no matter what."

I didn't know what to say. I sat there on my bed, staring at the MGS band, and it started to hit me that maybe this whole Mystical Guiding Manatee thing was much more advanced than I realized.

"Thank you Maynard," I finally said. "I will wear it every day, proudly and with honor."

Maynard's face lit up, and he said, "Jake I'm so glad you like it, but I don't think it's a good idea for you to wear it every day. It would probably be better if I kept it tucked away in my most secret pocket and you only wear it when we're getting ready to go on an adventure. We don't want people to start asking you all kinds of crazy questions about what it is and where you got it."

"You're absolutely right, Maynard. It's so unique that it will for sure catch people's attention, and I wouldn't know how to answer all the questions. So you keep it and give it to me when it's time; just don't forget which pocket you put it in, OK?"

"OK, that's a deal," Maynard said as he stuck out his flipper for us to shake on it.

Chapter Seven

Should we get this show on the road?" I asked as I picked Maynard up and headed to the bathroom.

"Absolutely we should!" Maynard agreed. "Let's get in the tub, and I'll send my signal to the Chief Vibrational Conch Blower. We'll have to wait about five minutes, give or take, for the signal to be sent back to my MGS, which will then send a signal to activate the vacuum system that will suck us into the drain. Easy-peasy!"

Well, I thought to myself, if it sounds easy-peasy to Maynard, and he understands how all of the signals work, then I'm just gonna climb into the tub and hold on!

"Is this about where I should sit?" I asked, as I made sure that my right leg was crossed over my left leg.

"Yep, that's perfect! Now, gently set me in the tub in front of you and about three inches from the drain hole. Now we just sit and wait."

"Maynard, what about your 'magical berries'? Don't you think it's time we start munching on them so we're ready when the signal comes through?"

"Jake, it's 'mystical' not 'magical'! Come on man, how many times do I gotta tell you?" Maynard said with a huff as he began the seemingly never-ending search for just the right pocket.

"I know, I know, I'm just messing with you." I said trying to calm Maynard down as he was clearly getting frustrated that he couldn't find exactly the pocket he needed.

"Ahh, here's the pocket I was looking for. I knew it was here somewhere," Maynard finally said.

"OK Jake, hold out your hand and I'll give you your four little berries. Oh, and if I were you, I would eat them all at the same time and really, really fast 'cause they taste a little yucky!"

"How yucky?" I asked.

"Well, I guess it depends on what you're comparing them to. They don't taste as good as an oatmeal-raisinless cookie, but they don't taste as bad as dog poop. Just quit being such a big baby, toss them in your mouth, chew them up really quickly, and swallow. We're wasting precious time sitting here talking about it, so pop and chew already!"

"You go first," I said, not having any confidence that Maynard was telling me the truth about how they taste. But come to think of it, with a name like the Yuckapouie plant, they probably taste horrible.

"Good grief, Jake!" Maynard said as he tossed his four little berries in to his mouth. It was what came next that made me almost climb out of the tub. Maynard's eyes slammed shut and started watering so bad I thought he was crying, and there was a little bit of purple foam coming out of the side of his mouth, his lips were pinched together really tight, and he was waving his flippers all around.

"See, easy-peasy!" Maynard announced as he wiped purple foam from his lips.

"Oh, that did not look 'easy-peasy', Maynard! You looked like you were trying to swallow dog poop!"

"Jake, stop talking and eat your berries! We gotta be ready at the same time when the signal comes. Now EAT!!"

So I popped those four little berries in to my mouth and everything seemed OK at first; they didn't taste bad, so maybe Maynard was just exaggerating to freak me out. And then I started chewing, and that's when all heck broke loose. The berries exploded in my mouth. It was absolutely, positively the grossest, nastiest, foulest taste in the whole entire world. And then the berry juice got foamy, and I was sure I was going to barf purple foam all over Maynard and the bathroom.

I started to panic that I was going to ruin the entire trip for us because I didn't know how I was going to swallow this foam. And then I finally felt Maynard grab a hold of one of my flailing hands and told me to swallow as quickly as I could and the awful taste would immediately go away. So, I plugged my nose and somehow swallowed. Thankfully Maynard was right: the horrible, nasty, foul taste was gone instantly!

"You OK, Jake?" Maynard asked as he jumped up on the counter and grabbed a bottle of water and tossed it to me.

"Uh, sure, I guess!" I said as I gulped down the entire bottle of water. "I gotta be honest with you, Maynard. I didn't know if I was going to be able to swallow all that purple foam because it was pretty gross. Why do they have to taste so bad?"

"Jake, just think about it for a minute: if the berries taste like delicious little candy bars, everyone would eat them all the time, and then everything would be in complete chaos; some would get small, then some would get large, then get small again, then large again."

"I guess you're right. It would be kind of weird. But you have to admit, it would be kind of funny to watch!"

"Uh, no it wouldn't," Maynard said as he rolled his eyes at me and settled back into his spot.

"Jake, now that we've eaten our berries, let's go over a few 'traveling rules'. The most important rule for you to remember is to not let go of my cape while we are in the Time Warp Tunnel, OK? This is rule number one, two, and three. The most important 'traveling rule' of all, got it, Jake?"

"OK, OK, I won't let go of your cape! Hey, Maynard, just for kicks, what will happen if I let go?"

I'm not quite sure why I even asked that question, 'cause I'm pretty sure I don't really want to know what will happen if I accidentally let go.

"Jake, I'm not gonna tell you what I've heard from the other manatees. It makes me kinda squeamish to think about it, but what I can tell you is that you could get trapped in some kind of time-warp-thingy, and then I would have to go back in and try to find you . . . I hear it can get pretty messy and yucky! So just DON'T LET GO, OK?"

"OK, I'll just hold on for dear life, I promise! But hey, if we do get separated, you'll come back and look for me, right?"

"Oh, Jake, don't you worry! I can't lose my very first assignment, now can I?"

"No, no, you can't! OK then, let's get this over with!" I said, with as much enthusiasm as I could muster.

"Jake, oh my gosh, wait a minute! I just thought of something!"

"Good grief, Maynard. What now?" I said a little harsher than was probably necessary.

"Hey, kid, all I was gonna say was why don't you go put on your bathing suit? It might be a little more appropriate than your pajamas. You really need to hurry 'cause our vibrational signal will be here any minute!"

"Gosh, Maynard, you scared me, but you're right. I wasn't even thinking about that! Don't disappear or do anything weird, OK? I'll be right back and don't leave without me!"

⁓

"Maynard? Maynard? Come on, man. Where are you? Would you please stop screwing around already! Maynard, did you leave without me? If you did, I'm never gonna talk to you again, and I'm not gonna go to your faraway island, no matter how much you beg! Then you're gonna have to tell King Ro Ro and Queen Hee Hee that you flunked out with your very first assignment!" I ranted to the bathroom walls.

"Gosh, Jake, I'm right here. There you go getting your panties all twisted in a knot again. And for the record, it's King Moo Moo and Queen Mee Mee. Please don't forget that; they will be so insulted if you call them some silly made-up names. I just had to go to the bathroom. No need to panic! Uh, Jake, you're the one who gave me that whole bottle of water, remember?"

"Yes, Maynard, I remember, but I thought you were gonna hold it. Anyway, can we go already? Have you called to tell everyone that we're coming?"

"Yep, I sure did! Everyone's over the moon to get to meet Jake the Snake!"

"Not you too. Everyone calls me Jake the Snake; can't you find another nickname? I'm so over Jake the Snake!"

"Well, OK then, never again will you be Jake the Snake. How about Jake the Grouchy Bear?"

"Maynard, oh my gosh, I almost forgot! I called my Grandma tonight to tell her about my big hit, and, well, I told her a little bit about you, and you will never, ever guess what she said."

"Hmm, let me think! I bet she went on and on

about how lucky you are, how happy she is for you, blah, blah, blah!"

"Oh my gosh, Maynard, how did you know all that? I know, I know, I keep forgetting about the 'mystical' part, right?"

"Yep! As soon as you start believing that I ain't no average manatee, then things will start to make a lot more sense to you!"

"OK, Mr. Smarty-Farty Pants," I said. "One more question. What's my grandma's name?"

"Come on, Jake. Ain't you got one harder for me than that? Your grandma said, 'Say hi to Maynard from Vicki-Lou!' Jake, come on, kid. Let's go before your head pops off your shoulders.

"Your blue light should be flashing like crazy! Hold on! Hold on tight, 'cause here we go!"

Chapter Eight

And then, down we went! And Maynard was right, my blue light was flashing like crazy. We flew through the drain ridiculously fast, so fast that my legs were flying out behind me, and it was all I could do to hold on to Maynard's cape. I didn't really mind the speed, that was kind of fun. I just didn't like the total darkness. I was very relieved when I saw the light at the end of the drain, but that relief didn't last long; I quickly realized that we weren't slowing down, and the light was getting closer and closer. I buried my head in Maynard's neck, closed my eyes really tight, and prayed that this crazy manatee knew what he was doing.

Sure enough, we didn't stop at the end of the drain but went flying through the air. I felt like an ant on the back of a tree frog. The effects of the Yuckapouie berries hadn't yet worn off; I felt incredibly vulnerable flying through the air in this little tiny body. I hoped we were heading toward something soft, but I was too afraid to open my eyes to find out. I don't know if we were actually flying because I'm not too sure if Mystical Guiding Manatees can fly, but what I do know is that we shot out of the drain like a cannonball. I knew that gravity would soon take over and hoped that Maynard had a landing pad in sight.

Reluctantly, I opened my eyes and was so relieved to see that Maynard had everything under control. Maynard handled the landing like a champion; he put us down right in the middle of a river. We skipped along the surface of the water a few times and then eventually came to a stop. It was a little bit of a bumpy landing but not too bad.

I quickly scrambled back to a comfortable place on Maynard's back, straightened his cape, patted him on the neck, took a deep breath, and looked around. The water was cool and perfectly clear. It was nighttime, and I was thankful there was a huge full moon that was incredibly bright. It was so bright I was able to see through to the white sandy riverbed that looked as if it had never been disturbed.

And then it hit me. The most intense surge of heat rushed through my entire body. It was so sudden and powerful that it knocked me completely off Maynard's back and into the cool water of the river. As if that wasn't enough to get my attention, I started to get sharp tingling sensations in my fingers and toes that quickly raced through my entire body and crashed into the top of my skull, nearly bringing me to tears. At one point, I felt like my hair was on fire and that my head was going to pop off my shoulders. Then, there was an incredible burst of energy that exploded out of my ears. The sense of relief from this explosion was the most intense feeling I think I've ever had in my life. In a matter of seconds, I was back to my skinny, scrawny self, or so I hoped. I took a few deep breaths and just floated on my back for a few minutes staring at the night sky. I reached up and felt my head to make sure I still had all my hair. I was a little worried that the surge of intense heat might have burned it all off, but, thankfully, it was all still there. I'm not quite sure how I would have explained that one to my mom. Then I started to wiggle my fingers and toes; everything seemed to be in good working order, except, oh my gosh, where was Maynard? It hit me that I was floating down the river all by myself; I couldn't see Maynard anywhere, so I did what any brave, self-confident kid would do — I started screaming.

"MAYNARD! MAYNARD! MAYNARD, WHERE ARE YOU?"

To my huge relief, there he was, lying on his back, flippers stretched out wide, floating right past me. He was staring straight up into the night sky and looked like he was in a trance. I figured he was probably getting ready to morph into his larger self, so I gave him a little space and floated down the river with him, still quite unsure what my Mystical Guiding Manatee was going to morph into. Maynard had been telling me over and over how amazing he is when he is his HUGE, AMAZING, BIG-BAD-BUFF SELF, but since I had yet to see it for myself, I had my doubts. And then it started; his wave of intense heat looked like it was a lot hotter than mine as steam started to rise from the water around him and then his entire body began to tremble and quiver. Suddenly he bolted upright and dove straight down into the cool water of the river and started swimming in a circle, slowly at first, and then faster and faster until his body was almost unrecognizable. He was circling so fast that the momentum shot him straight up into the night air where he exploded into his HUGE, AMAZING, BIG-BAD-BUFF SELF!

All I could do was stare with my mouth hanging wide open; he was really impressive and enormous. Then, as quickly as he had shot up into the night sky, he tucked himself into a ball and came crashing into the river, landing the biggest cannonball I had ever seen. As I waited for Maynard to return from the depths of the river, I realized that riding on Maynard's back to the Island of Kahwallawallapoopoo in the South Pacific Ocean was going to be much safer than I had anticipated.

As Maynard came to the surface of the water, he broke the silence of the night by yelling, "So Jake, what do ya think of my HUGE, AMAZING, BIG-BAD-BUFF SELF?"

"Maynard you are amazing. I can't get over how incredibly huge you are. I gotta be honest: I had my doubts but not anymore. You are really impressive! I can tell you one thing for sure: I'm not worried about our journey to Kahwallawallapoopoo 'cause I know I'm going to be completely safe riding on your back!"

Maynard puffed out his chest a bit and started smiling his big goofy smile.

"Well then, let's go!" Maynard announced. "Jake, climb onto my back, straighten out my cape, get yourself settled into a comfortable spot, and hold on, 'cause it's time to get through the Time Warp Tunnel!"

As we began floating down the river, I realized that it didn't have any of the usual stuff in it like fish, turtles, trees, shrubs, rocks, or seagrass. Although Maynard might have enjoyed a little nibble along the way, I was glad we didn't need to worry about floating into anything creepy, but it was still kind of strange.

As we started our journey down the lazy, winding river, we began to see things that were completely unexplainable. I tried to tell myself to just relax and not get freaked out, but what we saw next convinced me that this was a very different kind of place.

When we rounded the bend, we saw hundreds and hundreds of incredibly enormous rock formations. These weren't just big piles of rocks; they were perfect life-like statues of all types of wildlife. There were so many that it was impossible to believe that anyone could have carved them by hand. We saw an eagle, with its wings spread wide, perched upon a stone pillar; there was a gigantic elephant with a baby by its side; a magnificent lion; and dinosaurs from long ago. I can't even begin to describe them all; there were just far too many.

Good grief, I thought to myself, if this is the Time Warp Tunnel, this is a piece of cake. What's so hard about floating down a river?

"Jake? Jake, are you still back there?" Maynard asked.

"Maynard, of course, I'm still back here. This is so cool; why didn't you tell me it was gonna be like this? I could go through this Time Warp Tunnel every day, easy-peasy," I bragged.

"Sorry to burst your bubble, but this isn't the Time Warp Tunnel, goofball! This is how we get to the Time Warp Tunnel. That is the Time Warp Tunnel,"

Maynard said, as he pointed toward a gigantic pyramid that was looming in our very near future.

"Holy cats!" I shrieked. I wanted to ask Maynard if we could just float on past that pyramid and keep looking at all the cool statues and maybe do the Time Warp Tunnel another time, but I know he's really looking forward to going home. Plus, I didn't want him to think I'm a big scaredy-cat, again! I just needed to keep repeating to myself what my grandmother always tells me, *"Courage doesn't mean you don't get afraid . . . courage means you don't let fear stop you."* So, I kept my mouth shut and focused on figuring out how not be scared.

My parents have told me hundreds of times the best way to get through a scary situation is to look it right in the eye and do not back down, so I stared right at that gigantic pyramid. It wasn't really all that scary; it was just really, really big and had a really cool sunflower growing out of it, no big deal.

Actually, it was kind of a big deal 'cause this sunflower wasn't an ordinary sunflower — it was a real, living sunflower. The enormous dark-brown center looked warm and inviting, like a big mug of steamy, yummy, hot chocolate, but it was the hundreds of sparkly, bright yellow petals that were dancing and twirling and jumping all over the side of the pyramid that made the sunflower extraordinary. Come to think of it, the shade of the bright yellow petals was exactly the same color as Maynard's cape.

As we got closer and closer to the pyramid, we could feel the powerful energy force radiating from the sunflower, pulling us closer and closer. Even if we wanted to float past the pyramid, I don't think we could've. I'm pretty sure we were at the point of no return. I just had to believe that Maynard was as mystical as he said he was and that he would get us through the Time Warp Tunnel safely.

Maynard started to explain that we were going to enter the Time Warp Tunnel through the big dark-brown center of the sunflower.

"Oh, OK, that sounds cool, I guess. But Maynard, how are we gonna get all the way up to the big dark-brown center of the sunflower? I don't see any stairs or a ladder or a pathway anywhere."

"Remember when I said that you needed to hold on really tight to my cape and don't let go? Well, I wasn't kidding; getting to the dark-brown center of the sunflower is one of the trickiest parts of our Time Warp journey. In just a few seconds, the power of the sunflower is going to pull us up and push us through to the other side. Jake, you need to start relying on your MGS band because it's gonna alert you when a big change is coming so that you can get ready. You're gonna want to hold on super tight and don't let go, OK? Are you ready?" Maynard yelled.

"Uh, do I have a choice?" I yelled back.

"Nope!" was the last thing I heard Maynard say.

And just as Maynard promised, my blue light was blinking like crazy, again.

I realized the lazy winding river was starting to speed up. The water began to churn and swirl around us, and the wind began a steady howling as it too was picking up speed. Then the swirling became faster and faster, which created a waterspout that lifted us right out of the water and carried us up toward the dark-brown center of the sunflower. I looked down at my hands: my knuckles were white from the death grip I had on Maynard's cape. Maynard and I spun and whirled around and around and around. Poor Maynard; I flailed around like a rodeo cowboy, so I'm sure he's gonna have some bruises.

At this point, I'll admit, I closed my eyes and screamed like a baby. I was certain that Maynard's cape was going to cut loose and send me flying. If this happened, I knew there'd be no way that Maynard and I would be able to reconnect, and then, thankfully, the spinning and whirling began to slow down. Just as quickly as it had started, it was over. The spinning had stopped, and it felt like we were floating in a cloud.

I bravely opened my eyes and saw that we really were floating, not in a cloud, but in a tunnel. It was a tunnel of sparkly, golden-yellow weightlessness. Maynard playfully took full advantage of this freedom from gravity and started doing somersaults and backflips with ease while bouncing off golden walls of softness. Sounds from dolphins and whales singing filled the tunnel; I liked it in here. I hoped we could stay in here for a little while, but just as I caught my breath and my heart stopped racing, the blue triangle on my MGS band started blinking like crazy, and Maynard yelled for me to hold on tight because the sparkly, golden-yellow tunnel was coming to an end.

Sure enough, I could see that the tunnel was getting smaller and smaller until all I could see was a tiny ball of golden-yellow light. I didn't know how Maynard and I were going to get through that tiny ball of light, but sure enough, we squeezed through into yet another tunnel.

Our trip through the tiny ball of golden-yellow light thrust us abruptly back into gravity, which sent Maynard and me tumbling head first into this next phase of our journey. This tunnel was stark and cold, the complete opposite of the sparkly, golden-yellow tunnel. This sudden transition from zero-gravity made me feel nauseous and lightheaded. I rested my head on Maynard's neck and prayed that I wasn't going to barf all over his perfectly yellow cape. We could no longer hear the dolphins and whales singing; all we could hear was the howling of the wind and the waves of the ocean crashing around us.

This tunnel was made entirely of glass, which gave us an excellent view of the deep waters of the ocean, but it was just so different from the sparkly golden-yellow tunnel that it couldn't help but be disappointing. There was a powerful howling wind pushing us through this tunnel so quickly that it was impossible for Maynard and me to speak to each other.

Since we were moving so quickly through this tunnel, it was nearly impossible for me to see anything but water. I was starting to get a little scared and desperately wanted to talk with Maynard. I was tired and ready for this to be over. As I leaned forward to lay my head on Maynard's neck, I noticed that Maynard was waving his flippers around and tossing his head back and forth. He was definitely trying to tell me something; I had to pull myself together and figure out what it was that Maynard was trying to get me to see. I sat up as straight as I could, kept one hand gripped tightly to Maynard's cape and tried to use my other hand to block some of the swirling wind so I could find out what Maynard was desperate for me to see.

Finally, off in the distance, I saw what looked like road signs, which I think is what Maynard wanted me to see. I patted him on the neck and pointed to the signs and gave him a thumbs-up to let him know that I understood that he wanted me to read the signs. The first sign we came to read, 'Atlantic Ocean - Next Exit,' the next sign read 'Caribbean Sea - One Mile,' and then we saw what surely had to be our exit as the sign read, 'South Pacific Ocean - Five Miles.' Maynard again began waving his flippers around and tossing his head in the air; I was sure he was telling me to get ready because that was our exit. Then I remembered to check my MGS band, and sure enough, the little blue light was blinking like crazy, I was so relieved; this had to mean that our journey through the Time Warp Tunnel was almost over. I barely had a second to enjoy my relief when out of nowhere, and without any warning, Maynard and I were swarmed by hundreds of fish.

I don't mean just any kind of fish; these fish were about two inches long and some of the craziest looking fish I've ever seen. Everything about them was bright and colorful; some had blue bodies with bright orange polka dots; others had stripes of green and purple and pink; some were all blue with bright pink fins and orange lips; it was insane how colorful these fish were. Much to my relief, they were very friendly and playful, chasing each other, and bouncing around like puppies and kittens. Then, all of a sudden, they stopped playing and fell in line, one right behind the next. They formed a tight circle around us as we started to get close to our exit; it was as if they were creating a protective shield around us.

The next thing I knew, we took a sharp right turn onto the exit ramp that said 'South Pacific Ocean' and were thrust into a pitch-black tunnel at a very high rate of speed. I soon learned this was the shortest part of our journey. The next thing I knew, some unknown force launched us like a rocket into the cool night air for what felt like at least a mile up into the darkness. I have no idea how it was possible, but our protective shield of colorful fish had stayed intact. Just when I began to wonder how high up we were going to go, I felt Maynard round his back a bit and tip his head down toward the ocean, and we began our descent. I could feel Maynard begin to prepare for our entry into the ocean; he tucked his flippers tight to his body and stretched his tail out perfectly straight. I figured I better do what I could, so I lay flat on my stomach, my legs stretched down the length of Maynard's back, carefully let go of Maynard's cape, and wrapped my arms as far as they could go around his massive neck, and then we all dove deep into the South Pacific Ocean.

I could feel Maynard use his massive size and tremendous strength to get us to the surface as quickly as possible. He probably won't admit it, but I think he had a little help from our protective shield of colorful fish, as they were still in their tight circle around us. When Maynard and I reached the surface, we took a few deep breaths of the warm, salty air and watched as the colorful fish began to swim playfully around us, as if to tell us we were safe. Almost as if on cue, they all stopped dead in their tracks, paused for a split second, jumped straight up into the air as though to say goodbye, and then dove into the deep waters of the South Pacific Ocean.

"Maynard, are we done?"

"Yep, we're done, little buddy. We made it all the way through. Jake, I'm very proud of you," Maynard said.

"Aw, thanks, Maynard. It was pretty cool! It was a little weird at first and then a little scary, and then it was beautiful and amazing, and then weird again and a little scary again, but all in all it was pretty cool, I guess. My favorite part was the crazy colorful fish; for some reason they made me feel safe. And now, oh my gosh, here we are, right in the middle of the South Pacific Ocean!"

"So, Maynard, are we ready to go?" I asked, not too sure what Maynard's plan was or how long it was going to take to get to the Island of Kahwallawallapoopoo.

"Well, first things first, little buddy. I'll need a minute or two to work out some of the kinks! It's been a while since I've been my HUGE, AMAZING, BIG-BAD-BUFF SELF, but don't you worry, this shouldn't take too long! Roll off my back for a minute, will ya? I need to do some of my stretching exercises. Can you tread water for a few minutes?"

"Yep, I sure can. I was on a swim team when I was a kid, so you don't need to worry about me. Take all the time you need! I don't want you to pull a muscle or get a big cramp out here in the middle of the ocean. Hey, Maynard, what would we do if we did have a problem out here all by ourselves?"

"Oh, not to worry, Jake, I have lots and lots of friends I can call upon to help us out. The Mystical Guiding Manatees have quite a network of 'special helpers' in case of an emergency. Just a couple more barrel rolls, and I should be good to go."

Chapter Nine

Well, I guess that should do it. I think I've got all the kinks worked out," Maynard finally announced.

"Gosh Maynard, when I said 'take all the time you need', I didn't realize you were going to need an hour!"

"Hey, Mr. Smarty-Farty-Pants, a guy's gotta do what a guy's gotta do. I'll have you know it ain't easy being me. Sometimes I'm all squished into that little stuffed animal body and then sometimes I'm 'Maynard the Amazing'. Patience, young Jedi, patience; the transition to my HUGE, AMAZING, BIG-BAD-BUFF SELF is a very delicate process."

"All right already, I'm sorry. I didn't realize how very delicate you are, but now that I know, I will be so much more considerate of your delicateness!"

I swam over and quickly climbed on Maynard's back. I didn't want him to leave me out here by myself for laughing at him.

I leaned over and patted Maynard's neck, gave him the thumbs up sign, and told him I was ready if he was. He clapped his flippers together, tossed his head, and yelled, "Hold on tight, 'cause here we go!"

"GO, MAYNARD, GO . . . GO, MAYNARD, GO! Holy cats, Maynard, I can barely hold on . . . WOO-HOO! WOO-HOO!"

"Jake, you gotta hold on tight. . . . I'm gonna try one of my most impressive tricks. Here we go . . . !"

"Wait a minute, Maynard! Just hold on a minute!" I yelled, as I felt Maynard's powerful body beginning to pick up steam.

"Tricks? What kind of tricks exactly do you have?" I yelled, hoping that Maynard heard me in time to slow down.

"Well, Jake, I call it the BELLY-BUSTIN-KNEE-KNOCKIN MAYNARD SURPRISE!"

"Maynard, what did you just say?"

"I said, I call it the BELLY-BUSTIN-KNEE-KNOCKIN MAYNARD SURPRISE!"

"Good grief, Maynard. Why the heck do you call it that?"

"Because it's an amazing trick and my signature move. Believe me – it stops everyone dead in their tracks when they see me do it! I'll have you know, it's quite impressive that such a HUGE, AMAZING, BIG-BAD-BUFF manatee such as myself can pull it off with such grace and elegance. It proves my point that I am by far the most athletic manatee that lives in The Lagoon! So, Jake, can we do it? It'll be awesome. I promise, you're gonna love it!"

"BELLY-BUSTIN-KNEE-KNOCKIN MAYNARD SURPRISE! Well, it sounds a teeny bit terrifying, but let's do it. I'm sure it will be OK, right? It can't be any scarier than the Time Warp Tunnel, right?"

"Definitely! Absolutely! I've practically got this trick mastered. All I need is for you to sit tight and hold on, and I'll do all the work, OK? Are you ready?"

"Well, sure, I guess I'm ready. Hey Maynard, quick question, where exactly should I hold on? It's not like you've got a saddle on your back or a long, flowing mane for me to grab a hold of?"

"Good question, Jake. Excellent question! Hey, I'm sorry, I guess I got so excited about showing you my BELLY-BUSTIN-KNEE-KNOCKIN MAYNARD SURPRISE that I forgot to tell you about all of the cool stuff my cape can do. See, not only is it the most amazing color of yellow, but it can convert into lots of handy tools. For instance, it can become a seatbelt, so you won't fall off my back; or a life raft if we need a break from swimming; or a hammock if we want to take a nap; or a kite if we want to do some kite surfing. See Jake, the possibilities are almost endless."

"Gosh Maynard, why didn't you tell me about all the cool things your cape could do before we entered the Time Warp Tunnel?" I asked, a little sharply.

"Uh, I guess I should have done that. I just kind of forgot about it in all the excitement. I'm sorry. I'm really sorry, Jake."

"Oh Maynard, it's OK. At least you told me now. Let's convert this cape into a seatbelt and get me strapped in because I'm about ready to lose my nerve and call this whole thing off!" I said to Maynard, who seemed to realize that he better convert his cape into a seat belt pretty quickly or he was going to miss his big opportunity to show me his BELLY-BUSTIN-KNEE-KNOCKIN MAYNARD SURPRISE!

"Jake, is that better? Do you feel safer now? It looks like you are all secured and ready to go. Now can I do my BELLY-BUSTIN-KNEE-KNOCKIN MAYNARD SURPRISE? Please!!!!"

"OK! Let's go!" I shouted as I closed my eyes and said a quick prayer that this beautiful, perfectly yellow cape would do everything Maynard said it would and that this silly manatee knew what he was doing. Hopefully, a BELLY-BUSTIN-KNEE-KNOCKIN MAY-NARD SURPRISE was going to be half as much fun as Maynard said it was going to be.

"TAKE A DEEP BREATH AND HOLD ON TIGHT," was the last thing I heard Maynard yell.

We dove straight down in the South Pacific Ocean. Maynard took us down for what seemed like forever, then he turned and pointed his nose straight up, kept his flippers tight to his body, and began to spin like a top, all while pushing us up toward the surface with his powerful tail. We shot straight out of the water with incredible force; I felt like a cork popping out of a bottle. I was so thankful for the seatbelt. Even though we were no longer spinning, I'm sure I would've flown right off Maynard's back had I not been strapped in because of the speed we were going as we headed straight up to the clouds. Suddenly, I felt Maynard begin to bring his tail in toward his body, wrap his flippers tight around his tail, tuck his chin into his chest. Then we started to somersault, around and around and around, all the while plummeting rapidly down toward the South Pacific Ocean. Then, just in the nick of time, Maynard released his tail, spread his flippers wide, and did a pretty good impression of a swan dive right into the water.

"Good grief, Maynard. We got so high out of the water that I almost touched a cloud! But then, to be honest, I was a little worried you weren't gonna make that final flip at the end and that we were going to hit the water in the middle of one of the somersaults. But you nailed it, and we're still here to talk about it, so I guess it was safe enough, right?"

"Yep, Jake. It's completely safe! Well, maybe not completely safe, but safe enough, I guess. See Jake, the key to this trick is ya gotta make that last flip, 'cause if you don't make it all the way around, well then, you get a whole bunch of BELLY-BUSTIN-KNEE-KNOCKIN bruises and pains throughout your whole body! But hey, I've only had that happen two times, and surprisingly, I healed a lot faster than I thought I was going to!"

"Well, dare I ask how many times you've attempted that trick?"

"Well let's see, including the one we just did, that was my fourth time!"

"No way! That was only the fourth time you tried that trick, so that means that was only the second time you were successful? Oh my gosh, Maynard. Are you trying to get me killed?"

"Jake, no, I would never try to harm you. Were you scared? I didn't scare you, did I? That wasn't my intention at all! I guess I got a little carried away! I just wanted to show you my really cool trick, 'cause I'm the only Mystical Guiding Manatee in the whole world that can do that trick. I thought you would be really proud of me. You're not mad at me, are you?"

"No, I'm not mad at you. I know you don't mean any harm! You're just like a big, silly puppy sometimes! Hey, let's start heading toward Kahwallawallapoopoo. I'm ready to be there already," I said, loosening my new seatbelt so it wasn't quite so tight.

"Your wish is my every command, consider me your humble servant, your tour guide to the world, your . . . !"

"Come on Maynard, stop screwin' around, let's go!"

───

"Jake, we're almost there. I can see Kahwalla-wallapoopoo off in the distance. Can you see it?"

"Uh . . . I'm not sure."

After a few more minutes had gone by, I told Maynard that I still wasn't seeing an island anywhere out there. I started to wonder if maybe Maynard had gotten a little turned around after doing his BELLY-BUSTIN-KNEE-KNOCKIN MAYNARD SURPRISE. It's pretty dark out here; I guess it would be easy enough to get turned around.

"Hey, Maynard are you sure you're going the right direction?" I asked

"Ye of little faith," was all Maynard had to say as he continued to swim without hesitation toward his little island somewhere in the South Pacific Ocean. Maynard was swimming pretty fast, actually, quite a bit faster than I thought he could, but then I guess he is a Mystical Guiding Manatee, not just a run-of-the-mill manatee.

"Really Maynard?" I finally said. "Are you sure we're going in the right direction, 'cause all I see off in the distance is some really cool fireworks. Maybe it's a cruise ship that's having a celebration or something."

"Jake, that's not a cruise ship, silly! That's my home. That's Kahwallawallapoopoo in all her glory. I think I better slow down a little so that you can take a good look. It's pretty amazing isn't it?" Maynard said as he slowed way down so I could have a minute to take it all in.

"No way, Maynard. That's Kahwallawallapoopoo? It looks like they're having a celebration. Is it a holiday or is there a festival going on? Why all the sparkly lights and amazing colors; it's almost like on the

Fourth of July when you hold sparklers in your hand and wave them all around except about a thousand times more sparkly. How is it that there are so many colors all sparkling at the same time: purple, red, gold, green, silver, pink, yellow, orange . . . Maynard, that's really Kahwallawallapoopoo?"

"Jake, slow down, I can't keep up with all of your questions! First, yes, that really is the Island of Kahwallawallapoopoo. Second, no they are not having a celebration or a festival or a holiday; that's how Kahwallawallapoopoo always looks; well, I should say, that's how Kahwallawallapoopoo looks to those who truly believe in their dreams. If you don't truly believe in your dreams, then our island just looks like an ordinary little island somewhere in the South Pacific Ocean. But when you truly believe in your dreams, it's the most mystical place on the whole planet," Maynard said, full of pride that I could see Kahwallawallapoopoo in all her glory and thought his home was so spectacular.

"Hey Jake," Maynard said, quickly bringing us both back to reality. "I've been thinking, let's just go to The Lagoon today. I don't wanna take any chances getting you home on time; I wanna make sure we have plenty of time to get you back in your bed. First, I'll introduce you to King Moo Moo and Queen Mee Mee and then to all my brothers and sisters. Did I tell you that I have five siblings? I have a twin sister, Myrtle, and three younger brothers named, MacGyver, Maximus, Marlei, and my baby sis, Mandalay – Mandy for short. I also have tons and tons of cousins and gobs of friends."

"Slow down, Maynard, slow down. I can't keep up with all these names!"

"Oh, and I almost forgot . . . did I tell you that King Moo Moo and Queen Mee Mee are my mom and dad?"

"Uh, well, no. No, you didn't tell me that, Maynard! But that explains everything! That's why you're so nervous about not making any mistakes. Now I get it!"

"Jake, no screwing around. You gotta be on your bestest behavior. This is an important meeting for us, 'cause, you know . . ."

"I know, I know, I'm your first assignment! Maynard, relax! What's got you so worried? Are you afraid I'm gonna embarrass you or something? Hmm, so is it safe to say that you don't want me to tell your momma that you said the *fart* word? And hey, I'm just spit-balling here, but should I leave out the fact that you almost killed me doing your 'signature move'?"

"Please, please, please don't tell her I said that word, please! And just for the record, I did not almost kill you. You may have gotten a little bruised or banged up, but I definitely did NOT almost kill you. Jake, why do you need to mention any of that stuff, huh?"

"Hmm. Well Maynard, what's it worth to you if I stay quiet?"

"Good grief. Just go ahead and tell my mom. I don't care!"

"Oh, come on, Maynard, you big baby. Are you afraid of your momma? I thought you were all big and bad . . . you know, twelve-hundred pounds of solid muscle!"

"I'm not scared of nothin' Jake! It's just, it's just, I love my momma, and I don't like her to be mad at me, that's all! Hey, what about you? You still want your momma to kiss you good-night. See, I guess we both love our mommas."

"Yea, I guess you're right; we do both love our mommas. I promise I'm not gonna tell your momma any bad stuff about you! I was just kidding around! Come on, you big goofball. Let's go meet the gang, and I promise I'll be on my bestest behavior!"

Chapter Ten

Finally, after what seemed like forever, we arrived at the mystical Island of Kahwallawallapoopoo. Maynard swam right up to the edge of the coral reef. It was a perfect barrier for the calm, crystal-clear blue water of The Lagoon from the dark and unpredictable waters of the South Pacific Ocean. Even though it was nighttime, the bright light from the moon and the sparkly light from the hundreds of torches that lined the beach gave me a breathtaking view of the island and The Lagoon, but it was the spectacular color of the water that made everything appear mystical. Come to think of it, the color of the water was the exact same color as Maynard's eyes.

"Oh, Maynard, this is, I can't even think of a word to describe what I'm seeing! Even the word spectacular doesn't seem good enough."

"Jake, I tried to describe it to you, but as you can see, it's almost impossible to find the words to explain Kahwallawallapoopoo. It's just mystical, isn't it?"

"Maynard, it is mystical. What a wonderful place to call home! I might not want you to take me back to my home!"

"Jake, you haven't even said anything about the coral reef that we've been parked next to for the last few minutes."

And then I looked down. "Holy cats, Maynard, you're right. This coral reef is as spectacular as the island and The Lagoon!"

The coral reef was wider than I expected, probably half as wide as a football field, and was the shape of a perfect half-circle. Maynard explained that the coral reef is a living animal and home to thousands of creatures, including lobsters, clams, seahorses, sponges, sea turtles, sea snakes, hundreds of species of fish and sometimes even the shy reef shark, just to name a few.

As I studied the reef, I saw that the colorful fish who had escorted us out of the Time Warp Tunnel also made the coral reef their home. I guess they hadn't disappeared deep into the South Pacific Ocean after all; they too were on their way home.

And then, suddenly, the silence was broken by a loud chant.

"MAYNARD, MAYNARD! JAKE, JAKE!"

"Hey, Maynard, I kinda feel like a rock star with everyone chanting our names."

"I know. It's pretty cool, huh?" Maynard started yelling back. "Hello! Hello, everyone! We're home!"

"Jake, since you're my honored guest, you get to choose how we get from the South Pacific Ocean into The Lagoon. The first way is boring and traditional; there's a boring, predictable, and reliable tunnel that was created hundreds of years ago through the coral reef. We would dive down and just swim through the tunnel, and then we're in The Lagoon. Or, if you prefer, some of my buddies and I have invented a much grander entrance — one that requires a bit of athleticism, a bit of speed, a bit of height, and a little, teeny bit of courage. So which one will it be, Jake? You pick."

"Oh, thanks, Maynard! So my choices are safe and reliable or dangerous and unpredictable, right?"

"Well, kinda! But, Jake, I've done this grand entrance a whole bunch more times than I've done the BELLY-BUSTIN-KNEE-KNOCKIN MAYNARD SURPRISE, and I have had one, maybe two, little teeny mishaps. Jake, it's a real hoot! I know you'll have a blast!"

"OK, Maynard. What the heck? Let's go dangerous and unpredictable; why stop now? But are you sure you're not too tired? We've had a busy night so far, and you've been working pretty hard," I said, just a little concerned about how much Maynard still had left in his tank.

"WOO-HOO! WOO-HOO! Jake, we're gonna make it, I promise! I don't think I'm too tired; I think I'll be OK. Just a couple of things. Hold on real tight to my cape, tighten your seatbelt, and don't talk to me! I really, really gotta concentrate! I gotta get my timing just right so we make it completely across the reef, 'cause if I come up a little short . . . well, let's just say we might get a little bloody! And then I'm gonna get in big trouble for damaging the reef, so just sit real still, hold on, and don't say a word, OK?"

"Got it, Maynard! Let's just get this over with, 'cause you're starting to kind of freak me out! Go already; let's just get across this reef!"

"OK, kid. Here goes nothing! Just kidding, Jake, we're gonna fly like a bird in a few minutes! This will take a minute or two for me to get set up. We're gonna back up a little bit, so I've got plenty of room to get enough momentum to get us all the way across the reef."

"OH NO, DON'T DO IT, MAYNARD!" I heard someone in the crowd yell out. "DON'T DO IT, MAYNARD. DON'T YOU DARE!"

I started to sweat and think to myself, what if this crazy, goofy manatee gets us all scraped up and bloody? How will I ever explain that to my mom and dad in the morning? Maybe I should have just chosen the safe and predictable route, but it was too late to worry about that 'cause Maynard was starting to pick up speed. I could feel his powerful muscles under my legs really working to gain enough momentum to hurl us over the coral reef. I felt an overwhelming need to yell out encouragement, but Maynard said not to say a word. So, all I did was hold on and pray. Yes, I started praying like I've never prayed before! And then we were flying. Just like Maynard said we would, we were flying just like a bird. I carefully looked down to see if we had crossed over the coral reef yet and quickly realized we were starting to lose altitude. I mean, we were starting to fall like a brick, and we still had more reef to get across. I know Maynard said not to say anything, but just out of reflex, I heard myself start screaming, "GO, MAYNARD, GO!" I still don't know how we made it all the way across the reef, but we did. Not by much, but we made it!

"Whew, Jake, that was close," I heard Maynard groan. "Maybe I was a little more tired than I thought I was."

"Yeah, I know, Maynard. We just barely cleared the coral reef. It seemed like you were going fast enough in the beginning, but then about halfway across, we started to lose altitude very quickly. What do you think happened?"

"Well, Jake, I think I forgot to factor in the extra weight of having you on my back! I've never done that with a passenger before, so next time I'll just make a few little adjustments."

"Uh, next time, Maynard?"

And then we both heard someone yell, "MAYNARD, YOU BETTER GET OVER HERE RIGHT NOW!"

"Oh no, Maynard, your momma sounds madder than a box of frogs!"

"What am I gonna do? What if she doesn't let me be your Mystical Guiding Manatee anymore? Jake, I didn't scare you, did I? Will you tell her that you weren't scared and that we were just having fun?"

"Stop worrying so much. Of course, I'll tell your mom that I wasn't scared. Now stop worrying. Everything is gonna be OK, I promise!"

"Hello everyone! Hello, everyone, I'm Jake!" I yelled and started waving my arms, I felt like I should just take control of the situation so that maybe I could help keep Maynard out of trouble.

"Jake, what are you doing?" Maynard asked with quite a bit of panic in his voice.

"Maynard, I'm trying to keep you outta trouble. Just follow my lead! Now take me right up to your mom and dad and act like everything is OK!"

Maynard dutifully delivered me to his parents, and I wasted no time introducing myself. This is one of those times that I knew if I used my southern charm, it would keep both of us out of trouble.

"You must be Queen Mee Mee. Ma'am, it's so wonderful to meet you! And of course, King Moo Moo! Hello, sir. I'm Jake, and it is wonderful to meet you as well!" I said. I smiled, trying to hide my disbelief that I was really talking to a king and queen who were manatees in a lagoon of an island that was somewhere in the South Pacific Ocean.

King Moo Moo was enormous and engulfed his entire throne. His slick, bald, dark gray head had a hard time keeping his magnificent crown in place. The crown was exactly the same color as the blue water of The Lagoon, and there was a perfect sunflower centered right in the middle, just like the one on the pyramid at the beginning of the Time Warp Tunnel. It had the same warm, dark-brown center and sparkly, golden-yellow petals. There were small sparkly, golden-yellow triangles embedded all over the crown and round blue jewels at the top of each peak, also the same color of blue as the water in The Lagoon. His cape was just as enormous as he was and fell all around him and into the water. It looked like it was probably his favorite cape, as it had more than a few grass stains down the sides, and some of the feathers that lined the cape that were probably once quite magnificent were now matted — and many were missing altogether. It was a much-faded version of Maynard's bright yellow cape, but none of this seemed to diminish that King Moo Moo was, without question, the King of The Lagoon.

Although Queen Mee Mee's throne was the same size as her husband's, she wasn't nearly as large as he was. Her crown was exactly the same design as the king's, but she didn't seem to have any trouble keeping her magnificent crown in place. Her cape looked practically brand new; it was the same color as the blue water of The Lagoon, but it was the feathers that made it so spectacular. The feathers sparkled from the light of the torches, and the way they completely encircled her entire neck was something I had never seen anyone ever wear before.

After a few minutes of just sitting still on Maynard's back, I realized that I had probably been staring at the king and queen without saying anything for an awkward amount of time. But then I realized that they seemed quite content to sit quietly and allow me as much time as I needed to take it all in.

As I began to relax, even though nothing around me was the least bit normal, I began to realize that my grandmother was right; this was going to be the most amazing thing to ever happen to me. So, in my effort to help Maynard earn some big fat brownie points, I took a deep breath and began to describe how Maynard had bent over backwards to make our journey through the Time Warp Tunnel as safe and comfortable as possible. I went on to brag that Maynard was the best possible Mystical Guiding Manatee that a boy could ever have and I was probably the luckiest guy in the whole world; I couldn't possibly imagine my life without him.

I suddenly felt Maynard tapping me on the leg with his flipper and then I heard him whisper, "Cool it, Jake. You're starting to sound like a TV commercial for the Mystical Guiding Manatee Program."

"All right, already," I whispered back, "I'm just trying to help!"

"Jake dear," Queen Mee Mee purred. "We, the king and I, are so delighted to know that our dear, sweet Maynard provided you with a safe and comfortable journey through the Time Warp Tunnel. You know, dear, keeping you safe is one of Maynard's primary responsibilities, so the king and I are quite pleased to hear that our dear, sweet Maynard handled himself as a Mystical Guiding Manatee should. I must say, we are all so delighted that you and our dear, sweet Maynard were able to come to our beautiful island on such short notice. We have been eager to meet you in person. Our dear, sweet Maynard has spoken very highly of you and seems to be having the time of his life."

"Your Highness, please believe me when I tell you that having Maynard in my life has been an extraordinary experience! Maynard is kind and generous, and he makes me laugh until my belly hurts. But the best part about Maynard is that he is teaching me how to believe in myself when things aren't going my way. May I give you one example?"

"Of course, dear, yes, please tell us," the queen said as she adjusted her beautiful crown and settled back in her throne to listen to my story. It took a minute for me to begin my story because I was overwhelmed at how intensely the queen was looking at me. Something about her reminded me so much of my grandmother that it almost took my breath away. The queen's eyes were the same brilliant color as Maynard's, but it was the kindness in them that made me feel like I would always be safe here in her lagoon.

"You see, I play baseball, and I've been working hard to become a better hitter. I have spent hours and hours practicing, but when it's game time and I need to perform, I start to doubt myself. I start to dread my turn to hit, and the more I worry, the worse things get for me! A couple of days ago, I was having a miserable time during one of my games, and out of nowhere, this squeaky little voice calls out to me from my bat bag.

It says, 'Hey, kid! Yeah, you! Come here. I gotta tell you something!' So, I went over to my bat bag and found this squeaky little manatee waving his tiny little baseball cap around, telling me he knows why I'm not hitting the ball well and that he can help me. After a few minutes, I thought, well, what the heck? He certainly can't make things any worse for me, and this is what he told me: '*When you believe in your heart that you are ready and capable, then, and only then, will good things start to happen*!' And that's how I first met Maynard."

"So, tell us, did Maynard's wise words of wisdom help you hit the ball better?" King Moo Moo asked, as he leaned his large bulky body forward, greatly anticipating the outcome of Maynard's guidance.

"Yes, sir, they did! I hit my very first home run; I hit the ball clean over the fence, and we won the game!"

"Well, hallelujah, Jake," the king bellowed, an enormous smile engulfing his face. He leaned his bulk back in his throne, tossed his huge head in the air and began clapping his flippers together. "Oh, this is just wonderful news, Jake. Just wonderful! I'll bet you were so excited, and I am quite sure that your coach and teammates were happy as well. But, did you learn something about yourself? Do you understand what a powerful tool it is to believe in yourself? You hit that ball over the fence because you believed that you could, right? I would like for you to imagine, just for a minute, what else you will be able to accomplish in your life when you apply that same mindset."

"Your Highness, honestly, things have been so crazy since meeting Maynard that I haven't had time to think of it like that. But you're right: a tool as simple as believing in myself could mean that the sky is the limit, right? That my dream of playing for the Los Angeles Angels might not be such a silly dream after all?"

"That's right, Jake, you're absolutely right! You just keep believing in your dreams and yourself and I promise you, good things will begin to happen," the king insisted. He turned to Maynard and said, "Son, your mother and I are very proud of you. Your commitment to helping Jake understand and tap into his potential is precisely why we knew you would be the perfect Mystical Guiding Manatee for this assignment! Keep up the good work, son!"

"Thank you, sir! Thank you very much!" Maynard said. I couldn't help but notice how he quickly wiped a couple of tears away, probably hoping his father hadn't seen them.

Chapter Eleven

In her kind and soothing voice, Queen Mee Mee announced that we have an extraordinary guest joining us this evening.

"Jake, this is someone that we are very excited for you to meet. His name is King Peetar the Fifth, and he is the beloved leader of the WallaPoo people, with whom we share this beautiful Island of Kahwallawallapoopoo. Their village is a remarkable place. It is located on the other side of the island, an easy journey by seahorse. I'm expecting King Peetar to arrive any minute, so there isn't much time for me to explain why we want you to meet him, but trust me, all of this will make complete sense to you in good time," Queen Mee Mee quickly explained, all the while looking over her shoulder for King Peetar the Fifth's arrival

I tapped Maynard on the neck, hoping he could help me understand why I was being introduced to this King Peetar of the WallaPoo people, but he just shrugged his shoulders and smiled his goofy smile. Maynard doesn't seem too worried about this King Peetar and why he is coming for a visit, so I guess I shouldn't be either.

A rustling in the trees caught our attention well before we saw anything, and then we heard a kind voice say, "There, there, Rooney. Slow down. Right here will be just fine."

King Moo Moo's booming voice startled me as he welcomed this King Peetar person to their lagoon. When I looked up and saw King Peetar walking toward us, I couldn't believe my eyes. He was so young compared to King Moo Moo and looked like a professional athlete, like maybe he played baseball or football or something. I guess I imagined that he would be more like King Moo Moo, kind of old and large. Nope, not this king, no way.

"Well look here," announced Queen Mee Mee. "It is our very own King Peetar from the WallaPoo village. Peetar, it is so wonderful of you to come to The Lagoon this evening.

"Hello, Queen Mee Mee. You are looking as beautiful as ever! Is that a new cape? It's quite exquisite. It suits you well. Thank you so much for extending the invitation to me so that I might meet young Jake," King Peetar said as he bent down on one knee, bowed his head, and kissed Queen Mee Mee's flipper.

"Peetar, thank you for your kind words, and we are very honored that you made the trip to join us," Queen Mee Mee said as she smiled kindly at King Peetar.

"Ahh, Peetar, how are you? You sure are looking quite dashing these days," bellowed King Moo Moo. "Have those WallaPoo ladies found you a suitable wife yet?"

"Ahh, King Moo Moo, my beloved friend!" King Peetar said as he stood and moved to King Moo Moo's throne, bent down on one knee, and bowed his head for a moment.

"Your Highness," King Peetar said as he made his

way to a nearby throne that was obviously his. "With all due respect, please tell me that you aren't going to start asking me about finding a wife as well! Honestly, if I hear one more word about how it's time that I find a wife and start a family, I think I'll jump back on my Remarkable Seahorse and leave this island for good!"

"There, there, Peetar," Queen Mee Mee said in her most soothing tone. "Peetar, it's just that we all know you will make such an amazing husband and father. We hate to see you all alone in your big, beautiful house. Not to mention, we are also quite ready for little Peetars to run around the island, just like you used to. Do you remember, Peetar, how many hours you spent here in The Lagoon, playing all those silly games you would make up with all your manatee friends?"

"Of course, Your Highness. Those were some of the happiest times of my life . . . well, except when I was playing baseball, of course!" the king said, with a strange sadness in his voice.

"Well, of course, dear," said Queen Mee Mee.

"Excuse me, Your Highnesses," I said. "I'm so sorry to interrupt, but King Peetar, you played baseball?"

"Ah, this must be young Jake? The baseball player, I presume," King Peetar said as he looked over at Maynard and me with a big, welcoming smile on his face.

"Jake, King Peetar, please excuse our rudeness," Queen Mee Mee said. "Let me formally introduce the two of you! Jake, please allow me to introduce you to King Peetar the Fifth. He is the beloved king of the WallaPoo people. And yes, Jake, King Peetar was once an amazing baseball player!"

"King Peetar, sir, it is wonderful to meet you," I said as I sat up a little straighter on Maynard's back. I wasn't too sure if I was supposed to swim over and bow or what I should do, so I decided to play it safe and just stayed put, desperately hoping that I wasn't going to offend anyone. I wonder why Maynard never told me that there was a king on his amazing island who played baseball and looked like he spent all day, every day in the gym. I definitely needed to find out how he got so big, 'cause no matter how much I eat or exercise, all I ever see in the mirror is the same skinny, scrawny kid.

"Jake, I'll have you know that Peetar was, hands down, the greatest pitcher ever to come from the

Island of Kahwallawallapoopoo," declared King Moo Moo. "In fact, he was the greatest pitcher to ever come from all the South Pacific islands. He could throw a ball so hard that no one, and I mean no one, could hit it!"

"Oh, King Moo Moo, you exaggerate. I'm sure that someone must have hit one of my pitches!" King Peetar said. He seemed oddly uncomfortable talking about baseball and how good he once was.

"Well, that's not how I remember it," said King Moo Moo. "Queen, do you remember if you ever heard of anyone hitting one of Peetar's pitches?"

"Come to think of it, Moo, I think you're right!" said the queen. "His father had men come from near and far, just looking for someone to hit one of Peetar's pitches, and no one ever did!"

"Stop this nonsense, please," King Peetar begged. "Jake, I loved the game. I played the game with all my heart, and then, well, it was time for me to hang up my cleats. You see, there was, shall we say, 'a situation' that quite suddenly consumed me with far more significant responsibilities than just throwing a baseball. These new duties required all my time, which ultimately left no time for baseball. But, that was a long, long time ago. And speaking of time, I must head back to the village, as we have a council meeting this evening, and I shouldn't be late."

"Oh, Peetar, I hope we haven't upset you, but if you must go, we understand," Queen Mee Mee said. "Did Rooney bring you to The Lagoon?"

"Yes. Yes, he did! I always request Rooney; he knows this island as well as I do. I never need to worry that he is going to make a wrong turn that sends us deep into the forest!"

"King Peetar," I said, "thank you so much for coming to The Lagoon today so that we could meet. I hope that one day we can sit and have a long talk about baseball. I would love to hear some of your baseball stories."

"Jake, it was certainly nice meeting you as well, and I too hope that we can do that one day," King Peetar said, as he got up from his throne and made his way to King Moo Moo and shook his flipper and then kissed Queen Mee Mee on the cheek.

"Maynard," King Peetar said before he turned to leave, "you sure are all grown up. You look great, buddy. I can tell you've been working out with the weights. Take good care of Jake and safe travels."

"Thank you, Your Highness, and I will most definitely take good care of Jake," Maynard said proudly, as he puffed out his chest.

"Queen Mee Mee and King Moo Moo, thank you again for having me here today, and I will see you all very soon," King Peetar said as he walked to the trees where Rooney was waiting. We watched as he climbed on Rooney's back and rode off like the wind into the dense forest.

"Goodbye and safe travels," we all yelled and waved as King Peetar galloped away.

"Oh Moo," I overheard Queen Mee Mee say to the king, "I desperately hope that we haven't upset Peetar. It just breaks my heart when I think of all the sadness that has befallen him."

"There, there, Mee Mee, not to worry. I believe we have chosen well in young Jake. I'm quite certain, now more than ever, that he is just the person to help heal Peetar's broken heart."

"Yes dear, I am quite sure you are right," the queen said, as she leaned her head on the king's shoulder.

Chapter Twelve

other? Mother?" Maynard quietly called to the queen, who seemed very far away and in deep thought.

"Yes dear?" the queen finally replied, as she removed her head from the king's shoulder and sat up straight in her throne and tried to shake off her sadness.

"Mother, do you think this might be the right time to tell Jake about King Peetar?" Maynard asked. "I know Jake is dying to know why he was chosen to have a Mystical Guiding Manatee. And I can't think of anyone better to explain it to him than you and Father."

"Maynard, this needs to be entirely Jake's decision. Only he knows whether or not he feels ready to learn more about why he is here and why he was chosen to have a Mystical Guiding Manatee. We have already introduced Jake to quite a bit of new and exciting circumstances on this trip, so it might be best for us to wait a while to explain why he has been chosen to have a Mystical Guiding Manatee," Queen Mee Mee suggested while looking at me with the same kindness in her eyes that my grandmother always does.

"Oh yes, please, please, please tell me, Queen Mee Mee! I'm about to go crazy with all the questions I have! I promise, I'm ready to hear everything about why I'm here and why I was chosen to have a Mystical Guiding Manatee. There's no need to worry about me. I'm as good as gold; I'm as right as rain, I'm as . . ."

"All right, all right!" Queen Mee Mee laughed. "But do you boys think we have enough time to tell the entire story? We cannot have Jake getting back to his room late!"

"Yes, Mother, I think we have just enough time," Maynard said. "Mother, you can't even believe how fast I can swim now that I am so much bigger and stronger!"

"Yes, Maynard, I can see you have gotten considerably bigger and stronger, but we can't have you scaring the daylights out of Jake. We saw how you entered The Lagoon earlier, and we will most definitely be talking to you about that later, young manatee."

"Yes, ma'am, I understand, but there won't be any need to talk. I'll be careful, I promise."

"All right, son. Consider this to be your very last warning! Maynard, now please get your sister Myrtle. I would like her to hear this story as well."

"Yes, ma'am. I'll be right back," Maynard said. As soon as I slid off Maynard's back, he dove into the water and swam effortlessly over to where his sister was playing with her friends.

Queen Mee Mee motioned for me to come sit next to her. She quickly unfastened her spectacular cape and handed it to her husband.

"Jake, as you know, Myrtle and Maynard are twins; they have always been very close, and it will do them both some good to spend time together. I know they miss each other terribly, but I'm quite sure that neither of them would admit it. They are fiercely competitive with one another and much to Maynard's frustration, athletic events have always come extremely easy for Myrtle. That's not to say that Maynard isn't athletic, he is, but he just needs to work a little harder than Myrtle. The wonderful thing about the two of them is that they are always pushing each other to do their very best. They set the bar very high for themselves and are diligent about holding each other accountable."

"Queen Mee Mee, I completely understand. My cousin Kacey and I are very close as well. Sometimes so much so that I feel like we are more like brother and sister than cousins. Kacey and I aren't competitive with each other at all; we each stick to what we do best: she has her softball and photography, and I have my baseball, which keeps us both pretty busy. I wish she were here with me so I could share all of this with her. I know you would just love her."

"Oh, Jake, I'm sure we would love her, and you never know, we might just meet her one day," Queen Mee Mee said with a wink. I couldn't help but wonder what she meant by that, but just as I was about to ask her, Myrtle and Maynard surfaced right next to the queen and me, which kind of creeped me out, as I didn't even see or hear them swim up and had no idea they were so close to us.

"Here we are," Myrtle said as she playfully splashed water at Maynard, who then splashed water right back at her. It was obvious they were very happy to be able to spend time together.

"Well, Jake, it's wonderful to finally meet you," Myrtle said, as she swam over to me and nudged me playfully with her thick, powerful nose.

"It's so good to meet you as well, Myrtle," I replied and splashed a little water in Myrtle's direction.

"You shouldn't have done that!" I heard Maynard chuckle as he quickly dove under the water.

"Oh, Jake, two can play that game!" Myrtle squealed as she spun around and began splashing me with her powerful tail.

"OK, OK, I give up!" I laughed as I flailed around in the torrent of water Myrtle was sending my direction.

The next thing I knew, I felt Maynard swim under me and toss me in the air like a beach ball.

"Children, enough!" Queen Mee Mee said, trying

to hide her laughter. "We are wasting precious time with all this silliness. Now settle down so we will have time to tell you this story before Jake and Maynard need to leave."

"Yes, ma'am," we all said. Myrtle swam over to her father and leaned up against his throne, and I stretched out on Maynard's back.

"Now, this story goes back a long, long time. You see, when King Peetar the Fifth was just a young boy, he didn't have a care in the world. He was free to roam the island with his WallaPoo friends and play in The Lagoon with his manatee friends. Life was good. There were very few things that worried the young prince. Don't misunderstand, the prince knew that one day he would take the throne and become His Highness, King Peetar the Fifth. But what none of us knew, and to our complete dismay, was that it was going to happen much, much sooner than anyone had ever anticipated," Queen Mee Mee said as she looked over at King Moo Moo with tears in her eyes. King Moo Moo reached out his flipper and gently patted her on the back.

"The prince's father was King Peetar the Fourth. Peetar the Fourth was a beloved king and had a beautiful wife, Queen Cynthia. They were a perfect match and adored each other. They were smart, hardworking, healthy, compassionate, and loving people. They loved the Island of Kahwallawallapoopoo and all of its many inhabitants, but more than anything, they adored their only child, Peetar the Fifth. The prince was a very athletic child from an early age; he never played with any toys like the other children. He would only play with balls — baseballs, footballs, soccer balls, basketballs, tennis balls. If he couldn't kick it, throw it, or bounce it, he wasn't interested! Later, the king and queen were often overheard saying that maybe they should have insisted that the prince play with some of his other toys; or, perhaps they shouldn't have allowed him to go to his first baseball game on the Island of Kookapouee when he was at such an impressionable age.

"Needless to say, he became quite good in all sports, but as he matured into his teens, baseball became his true love, and boy, could he play. He loved to pitch, and I'm telling you, Jake, he had an arm like a lightning bolt. He could throw so hard and with such accuracy that it was rare when anyone could hit his pitches! The king and queen were quite proud of the prince's abilities and loved to watch him thrive at the game he loved. The king had a pitching mound constructed and a tire swing hung, and the prince would throw baseballs, footballs, anything he could find through that hole in the tire swing, hour after hour. Jake, as we said before, it got to the point where none of the men, young or old, on the island could hit any of his pitches. Isn't that right, Moo?" the queen turned and asked King Moo Moo.

"Yes, dear," the king replied. "That's how I remember it as well."

"So, King Peetar the Fourth did what any loving father would do: he sent some of the WallaPoo men out to neighboring islands in search of anyone who would come to the island and try to hit one of the prince's pitches. They came by the boatload, all types of men – young men, old men, large men, small men, fierce hunters, men who could catch fish with their bare hands – all types of men came and left without hitting a single pitch!

"King Peetar the Fourth and Queen Cynthia soon realized that the prince had an exceptional gift, which they knew could possibly be both a blessing and a curse. Word eventually spread to the Island of Kookapouee that there was a young future king who had a golden arm, a 'real lightning bolt', they would say. And then the inevitable happened: a formal announcement was delivered to King Peetar the Fourth and Queen Cynthia requesting that the young prince come to the main island to demonstrate his pitching ability to none other than the Kookapouee National Team.

"Jake, this request by the Kookapouee National Team created a complicated dilemma for the king and queen. They desperately wanted the prince to follow his dreams, no matter where it might take him, but the prince was the only heir to the throne. King Peetar the Fourth and Queen Cynthia were obligated to prepare the prince to become King Peetar the Fifth so he could fulfill his duties to the WallaPoo people. The king and queen were in excellent health and relatively young, but there was much to teach the prince. The traditions and customs of the WallaPoo people were centuries old, and there was much to learn to ensure the preservation of the WallaPoo community.

"Children," the queen said as she looked each one of us in the eye, "the manatees of The Lagoon and the The WallaPoo people rely on each other for the survival of our beautiful island and our two communities. If one or the other begins to weaken and deteriorate then it is very likely that it will be the end of both of our communities."

"Although King Peetar the Fourth and Queen Cynthia traveled to the Island of Kookapouee many times, they hadn't paid much attention to the Kookapouee National Team. They were busy attending annual summits with the surrounding island nations, shopping for goods to bring back to their tiny island, and, most importantly, maintaining friendly relations with the king and queen of the Island of Kookapouee. So, they had only attended a few baseball games, but mainly so they could bring the young prince back souvenirs. The prince always loved to get a new jersey or a hat, but what he liked most was information about the team: their stats, their training routines, and anything else he could get his hands on. He just loved reading everything about the Kookapouee National Team.

"Even though the prince was a tremendous pitcher, this request from the Kookapouee National Team was something that neither the king or queen had imagined possible; no one from the Island of Kahwallawallapoopoo had ever been summoned by the Kookapouee National Team for a tryout. Thankfully, one of the king and queen's trusted advisors had a little understanding of this request. The advisor explained that the Kookapouee National Team is an organization made up of young men in their late teens and early twenties who travel the world playing baseball games against other countries' national teams. These young men train and play in hopes of one day playing baseball in the United States for a Major League team. Upon hearing this explanation, the king and queen were even more conflicted than ever on how to proceed.

"Rumor has it," Queen Mee Mee continued, "that the king and queen struggled mightily with how to proceed until finally, after much discussion with their trusted advisor, they agreed to travel to the Island of

Kookapouee to meet with the representatives of the Kookapouee National Team. They would listen to what the coaches had to say, tour the training facility, and get answers to their many questions so they could decide how to proceed, once and for all!

"The travel date was chosen, and the prince was summoned to the king and queen's office. It was time to have a heart-to-heart discussion with the prince about this request from the representatives of the Kookapouee National Team.

"Upon hearing of this request by the Kookapouee National Team, the prince immediately begged his parents to let him attend the meeting. The king and queen adamantly refused and explained that WallaPoo protocol dictated that since young Peetar the Fifth was the only heir to the throne, the entire royal family could not travel together in case of a tragedy. The king explained to the prince that he and his mother would travel to the Island of Kookapouee to speak with these 'baseball people' and when they returned home, they would inform him if he would be allowed to travel to the Island of Kookapouee and demonstrate his abilities.

"And then, tragedy struck," the queen said as she bowed her head and reached for King Moo Moo's flipper.

"NO!" I yelled, as I rolled off Maynard's back and swam over to the queen's throne. "What happened? Peetar was so excited to try out for the Kookapouee National Team. Did he break his throwing arm? I don't understand. What do you mean that tragedy struck?"

"Oh, Jake, if only it were that kind of tragedy; this was a tragedy of epic proportion," Queen Moo said with tears in her eyes. "The king and queen set out on their voyage as planned. It was a beautiful day; there wasn't a cloud in the sky. Everyone was certain they would have smooth sailing for the four-hour journey to the Island of Kookapouee. Well, as it was fated to happen, the king and queen's ship was overtaken by what we assume was a rogue wave. Jake, these waves are unpredictable and massive in size; it most likely struck the ship so suddenly that no one had time to get to the lifeboats, and it more than likely took down the ship within a matter of minutes. Thankfully, the captain was able to get a distress call out to the

Island of Kookapouee. But by the time the Island of Kookapouee Coast Guard reached the area where the distress call had come from, the seas were calm, and there was no sign whatsoever that there had been a ship on the water.

"Children, when those coast guard ships pulled into our port and told us of the terrible tragedy that had befallen our beloved king and queen, our entire island went into mourning. The sadness we all felt was, at times, almost unbearable. Not only did we mourn the passing of our beloved king and queen, but we also regretted all that was lost for young Peetar. We all knew that it would be hard for him to pursue his dream of pitching for the Kookapouee National Team. We also knew that young Peetar would feel like he should step in where his mother and father had left off and assume the responsibilities that he was destined for from birth.

"As best we could, we all poured our efforts into the young king to help him transition from a young man who was full of dreams of another kind into the king of a small island full of people who needed his guiding hand. We all hoped that once young King

Peetar the Fifth began to heal from the tragic loss of his parents, he would take the advice of his father's trusted advisors and temporarily 'hand over' the reins of responsibility to a chosen advisor. Everyone believed that King Peetar the Fifth needed time to grow and mature. What better way to do that than to pursue his dreams of playing the game he loved. And then, much to everyone's surprise and complete dismay, young King Peetar the Fifth demanded that his tire swing and pitching mound be taken down and removed from his sight. He declared that every single baseball glove, bat, and anything else that reminded him of baseball was to be boxed up and put away.

"Children, little did we know, from that day forward, there would never be another game of baseball played on our beautiful Island of Kahwallawallapoopoo.

"We all hoped and prayed that this decision to banish baseball from the island would be a temporary one, but as time passed, the king became more and more adamant in his resolve. For a while, the king's closest friends and advisors pleaded with him to allow the children to play baseball. We all hoped that if the king saw the children playing baseball, it would somehow help him and the Islanders complete the healing process, but the king could not be convinced and held steadfast in his resolve. We have all watched how this unwavering opposition toward the game he once loved has taken a toll on him.

"Children, ever since that fateful day, a sense of sadness has lingered over the king, the WallaPoo people, the Mystical Guiding Manatees, and all the creatures of the island. There is a hole in everyone's heart that has yet to heal," the queen said as she closed her eyes and bowed her head.

"Life is like a baseball game: when you think a fastball is coming, you gotta be ready to hit the curve"

- JaJa Q. -

Chapter Thirteen

We all sat there in complete silence after Queen Mee Mee finished telling the story of King Peetar's tragedy. I looked over at Myrtle and tears flooded down her cheeks; Maynard's eyes were closed, and his head rested on his chest; I swam back over to Maynard and climbed onto his back. I just lay there in complete disbelief that something so horrible could happen to such a wonderful family.

"Oh my gosh, this is the saddest story I've ever heard! My heart is just breaking for King Peetar! I can't even begin to imagine what life would be like if I lost both of my parents at the same time and then found out that I would never play baseball again. I think that I too would be sad for the rest of my life."

"Jake, honey, yes, this is a very sad story, but it is not healthy to be in mourning for the rest of your life. It is important to honor those who have passed by living your dreams and building the life that they would have wanted you to have. This tragedy happened long ago, and our little island has mourned for a long time now. Peetar must join the living and put this tragedy to rest," Queen Mee Mee explained.

I looked at Queen Mee Mee with tears in my eyes, wondering why she had just told us this terribly sad story. I was even more confused as to why I was here and how this could possibly have anything to do with me. And then, like a ton of bricks, it hit me!

"You want me to help heal King Peetar's broken heart, don't you?" I blurted out.

"Ahh, young Jake," King Moo Moo said, "you are a very wise young man. I knew we had chosen well when we decided upon you. You see, we all love to watch you play baseball! You play with that same magic that King Peetar once played with."

"Oh my gosh, all of you have watched me play baseball? Hmm. How exactly have you watched me play baseball?"

"Jake, right now those details are not important. What is important is that I finish telling you why you are here. Don't forget, we must get you back to your bedroom very soon," the queen insisted.

"OK, you're right, but it's still a little creepy that you all have watched me play baseball, and I didn't even know it!"

"Jake, we know how much you love the game, how dedicated you are to improving your skills, and how hard you train. We have also seen how you've handled adversity on multiple occasions. We have seen you persevere through many difficult situations and continue to come through stronger and better. For these reasons, Jake, we feel that you are the perfect young man to help heal King Peetar's heart and bring baseball back to the Island of Kahwallawallapoopoo."

"Queen Mee Mee, King Moo Moo, I certainly don't mean any disrespect, but I don't understand how I could possibly do all that you are asking! I can't even begin to imagine how I could be the one person who could change King Peetar's mind!"

"Jake, honey," Queen Mee Mee said kindly, "I know we have overwhelmed you with information today. We – King Moo Moo, the elders, and I – have been studying you for a long time, and we are convinced, now more than ever, that you are the perfect young man for this task. We are certain you will have many questions in the days to come, so why don't you and Maynard go back home and get some rest. Talk things over with Maynard and, of course, your grandmother. Then you can make another trip to Kahwallawallapoopoo so we can talk about some of your concerns and see if we can come up with a plan that will work for everyone. Jake, Maynard, how does that sound?"

"Oh, Queen Mee Mee, that sounds like a great idea, 'cause I'm starting to get really tired. But before we go, may I ask you just one quick question?"

"Of course, Jake," Queen Mee Mee said, "anything at all."

"I am beginning to think that my grandmother may know more than she is telling me about

Kahwallawallapoopoo. Will you please tell me how you know my grandmother?"

"Oh, Jake, you dear, sweet boy. I know this must be quite unsettling for you to have so many questions and so few answers, but as I told you earlier, timing is everything. Trust me; you will learn all you need to know, all in due time!"

"Well then, I guess I'll wait! Thank you for not being mad at me for my hesitation. It's just that I, I don't, uh . . ."

"We know, Jake. You don't want to disappoint us, right?"

"How did you know that?" I asked, knowing I was way too tired to understand any answer the queen could give me.

"Young Jake, you keep forgetting that we are not just run-of-the-mill manatees. We are Mystical Guiding Manatees who care about you very much."

"I'm sorry. I do keep forgetting about the mystical part! OK, we'll come back in a few days, I promise!"

"We know you will, Jake. Travel safe, you two, and, Maynard, do everything by the book on the way home. Jake is too tired for any of your antics!"

"Yes, ma'am! Come on, kid. Let's go. I'll have you back in your bed in no time.

"Mother, may I please jump over the coral reef? I promise to be super careful! Jake will be perfectly safe, please!"

"Jake, dear, is it all right with you if Maynard jumps over the coral reef?" the queen asked me.

"Yes, ma'am. I trust Maynard completely to get us over the coral reef without any problems."

"Well then, go ahead, Maynard, but be extra careful; we wouldn't want either of you to get hurt or for our precious coral reef to get damaged in any way."

"Thank you, Momma, I promise I'll be careful," Maynard said and blew his mom a kiss.

"Goodbye, Mother. Goodbye, Father. Be good, Myrtle the Turtle. Thank you for everything. Love you and miss you already," we both yelled as we swam toward the coral reef.

"Wow, what a wonderful trip this has been. I'm so glad you brought me here to Kahwallawallapoopoo. It's more incredible than I ever could have imagined. Gosh Maynard, I'm exhausted all of a sudden; one minute I was fine, and now I'm getting so tired."

"Don't you worry kid, I've gotcha covered. Mom and Dad warned me that the Time Warp Tunnel can have a weird effect on kids. Just sit back and take a little cat nap while I get us to the entrance of the Time Warp Tunnel. I'll wake you when it's time to start our journey back through. Don't you worry about a thing; I've got everything under control."

"Are you sure you'll be OK, Maynard?

"Yep, I'll be just fine. Good-night, Jake," Maynard said.

"Good night, Maynard," I said, just as we were flying over the incredible coral reef. Before I settled in for my nap, I quickly peeked over Maynard's shoulder to make sure we were going to make it all the way across, and this time, Maynard nailed it; there was plenty of room to spare. I was pleasantly surprised to see that the colorful fish were all lined up and ready to join us on our journey to the Time Warp Tunnel.

This truly is an amazing place.

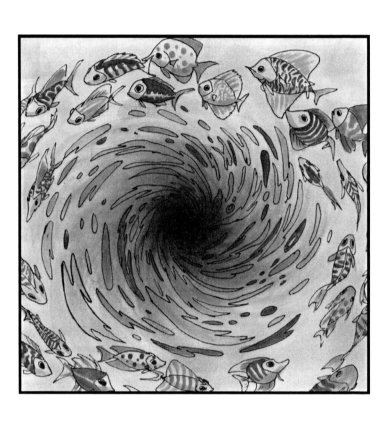

Chapter Fourteen

Hey, Jake. Jake, it's time to wake up. We're almost ready to enter the Time Warp Tunnel. Jake, it's time to wake up!"

I could hear Maynard calling my name and trying to get me to wake up, but I was so tired that I just wanted to ignore him and keep sleeping. Not to mention, I was dreading the journey back through the Time Warp Tunnel, with all of the twists and turns, spinning and floating. I just wanted to be back in my bed, sound asleep, with Bunny curled up beside me. Maybe if I just ignored Maynard a little longer, he would just go ahead and enter the Time Warp Tunnel and let me keep sleeping.

"JAKE, JAKE, you've got to wake up, right now! We're almost at the point of no return. Come on, Jake. You've got to wake up so that you can hold on. I don't want you to go flying off my back and end up in some tunnel that might shoot you off into the Dead Sea or someplace scary where I'll never be able to find you. Come on, man; please wake up!"

"WHAT, shoot off into the Dead Sea?" I screeched. "You mean that could really happen?"

"Well, look who's finally awake! It's Rip Van Winkle, and Grouchy Bear Jake, all rolled into one," Maynard teased.

"Maynard, I'm sorry that I yelled at you. I'm not a grouchy bear, I'm just really, really tired and really dreading going back through all of the tunnels and water spouts and the lazy river. I just want to be in my bed. Maynard, I know I sound like a whiny baby, but I gotta go to school tomorrow and to practice. Is there possibly a different tunnel that we could use?" I asked as I laid my head back down on Maynard's warm, soft neck and prayed that he knew of a much simpler and faster way for us to get home.

"Actually, yes! There is a different way for us to get home."

"WHAT? What did you just say?" I screeched as I bolted upright and slid off Maynard's back and swam around to look him in the eye. "Really, you mean there's a way for us to get home a whole lot faster than how we got here? Maynard, look me in the eye and tell me you're not kidding! Please tell me there really is a way," I begged.

"OK! OK, already! But please go sit back down; you're much safer on my back. It's called the Emergency Time Warp Tunnel. Sometimes a young person and their Mystical Guiding Manatee need to get back home in seconds, not minutes. You see, when a young person and their Mystical Guiding Manatee go on their adventures, they usually have a Guardian that helps make it possible. The Guardian's main responsibility is to provide an alibi for the young person and their Mystical Guiding Manatee when they leave the house to go on their adventures. The Guardian must keep the parents distracted from noticing that their son or daughter has disappeared for a while.

Jake, as you can probably imagine, this can be a very challenging task for a Guardian, as they must be very careful what they tell the parents and be very aware when it's time to call the adventures to an end. The Guardian and the young person each have a special whistle; if the Guardian needs the young person to come home immediately, they will send out a series of toots as a signal that they better get home as fast as they can. That's why the Emergency Time Warp Tunnel was created."

"Woohoo, woohoo!" I began to yell. "Let's find the Emergency Time Warp Tunnel and get back to my bedroom."

"Hold on there, little buddy, there's just one little, teeny, tiny thing that I've got to warn you about. Are you ready?" Maynard asked.

"Well, probably not, but go ahead," I said, as I slumped over Maynard's neck, holding my breath in anticipation that Maynard was going to tell me something horrible about this Emergency Time Warp Tunnel.

"Well, there are three things about this Emergency Time Warp Tunnel that you're not going to like: it's super-fast, super-dark, and super-cold. But, the good thing is, it doesn't last for very long, and it's a straight shot right to your bathtub. We stay in this same tunnel the entire time, and there's no water, just super-fast, super-cold air pushing us through the tunnel. So, what do you think?" Maynard asked as we were swimming slowly around in circles with the colorful fish following very closely behind us.

"Super-fast, super-dark, and super-cold" I repeated out loud. "OK, Maynard, let's do it. I'll be fine; we can do it. Just strap me in extra tight, and if you're not scared, then I'm not scared."

Maynard gave me a few pointers on how to strap myself in, and when I was ready, I patted him on the neck and gave him the thumbs up sign.

"It won't be long now. Jake, this is probably a good time for us to eat our berries 'cause we're just waiting for the colorful fish to find exactly the right spot to create the circle for us to dive into that will take us right into the Emergency Time Warp Tunnel," Maynard said.

"Maynard, honestly I don't think I'm gonna be able to swallow those berries; they just taste too disgusting, and that purple foam totally freaks me out. I'm pretty sure this time I'll probably throw up purple foam all over both of us. Please tell me that there's another way to get us small enough to fit through the drain."

"Well Jake, I guess if you can't eat the berries then we'll need to head back to Kahwallawallapoopoo. I don't know of any other way to get us small enough to fit through the drain, and I don't want to spend the night out here in the ocean. It's getting cold, and the waves are starting to get bigger, so hold on and I'll turn us around."

"What do you mean, head back to Kahwalla-wallapoopoo? We can't do that! I gotta go to school tomorrow and practice, and you know my mom will freak out if I'm not in my bed when she comes in to wake me up."

"So what's the plan, Stan?" Maynard asked, quite a bit calmer than I expected him to. "It's your call, Jake. I'll do whatever you want, but I'd like to ask you something: are you really going to let a few minutes of discomfort keep you from doing something amazing?

"Maybe this will help," Maynard added. "When I was younger and would complain about doing something that I didn't want to do, my mom would stop what she was doing, look me straight in the eye, and say, *'When you change the way you look at things, the things around you change'*. Jake it took her saying that to me about a million times before I finally realized that she is one hundred percent right.

"So, Jake, how do you want to look at this situation: as a small problem with an easy solution or a giant problem with no solution?"

"You're right, Maynard; you've made a good point. Sometimes you have to take the good with the bad. Will you please hand me four berries so that we can get home?" Gosh, I thought to myself, sometimes that goofy manatee really knocks one out of the park.

"Yes sir, four berries it is. And, I even stashed a bottle of water in one of my many pockets for you, so pop them in, enjoy the foam, take a big gulp of water, and wash everything down, easy peasy!"

"Thanks for the water, Maynard," I said. "So, what are we waiting for?"

"Well, when you see the colorful fish begin to form a circle and start swimming around really, really fast, that will be our signal that they are ready. This will be just like when we jumped over the coral reef, except this time I will be jumping right into the middle of the circle that the colorful fish create. Then we will shoot right into the Emergency Time Warp Tunnel, and we will be in your bathtub within seconds."

"OK, that sounds easy enough," I mumbled. All the while I wondered how much longer it was going to be until the colorful fish would find exactly the right spot to create the circle so we could enter the Emergency Time Warp Tunnel. Just as I started to doze off, I noticed the blue light on my MGS band blinking like crazy and heard Maynard yell, "Get ready, 'cause they're starting to spin!"

I leaned over and quickly splashed some cool water on my face so I could be as alert as possible for this final leg of our journey. Then I felt Maynard's powerful body working hard to pick up speed so he could launch us squarely into the middle of the colorful fish. I took a deep breath right before we dove.

It was incredibly dark, darker than anything I had ever experienced before, and we were moving so fast the skin on my face felt like it was going to peel off. And something else was happening: I was getting really,

really cold, like, down to my bones kind of cold. My fingers were stiff, and when I tried wiggling my toes they wouldn't even move. I started to worry that by the time Maynard and I popped out of the drain, we would be a solid block of ice. How was I going to explain that to my mom when she came in to wake me up for school?

I had no idea what time it was or even how much longer this Emergency Time Warp Tunnel was going to last. Then, to my huge relief, we were done. We were in my bathtub.

But there was a big problem: when I tried to slide off Maynard's back, I couldn't. My hands and legs were frozen to Maynard's super-cold cape.

"Hey Maynard, it looks like we're frozen together," I struggled to say since my teeth were chattering so hard. "I know you said the Emergency Time Warp Tunnel was going to be super-cold, but I didn't think you meant we were going to turn into ice cubes."

"Jake, we're gonna be OK, I promise. Let's just start thinking really warm thoughts, and I'm sure all of this ice will melt in no time."

"Really, Maynard? That's your solution to solving our ice problem?" I said shaking uncontrollably.

"No, Jake, I'm just kidding; warm thoughts are definitely not going to help. But as soon as you start to morph into your larger self and I start to morph into my stuffed-animal self, the ice will melt away and we will be perfectly fine," Maynard said, his teeth chattering, and his body shivering as much as mine were.

"Maynard, I think I'm getting ready to morph," I yelled as loud as my little self voice would allow. And then it hit me. Thankfully the morphing process wasn't quite as violent as the first time; I still got the surge of heat rushing through my body, which quickly melted the ice that had built up on Maynard and me. Then the sharp tingling sensations began to race throughout my entire body, and once the burst of energy exploded through my ears, POOF, I was big again.

I quickly stepped out of the tub and waited for Maynard to morph into his stuffed animal self. Thankfully, his morphing process wasn't nearly as dramatic as the last time either. Probably because he only had to morph into his little stuffed animal body.

"Gosh Maynard, it sure is good to be home. I'm pooped. How about you? I asked Maynard as I was getting us some towels so we could get dry and get to bed.

"Uh, ya Jake, I'm pretty pooped as well. Hey, give me your MGS band so I can tuck it away. It'll charge in my pocket and do any necessary updates," Maynard said.

I watched as Maynard found the pocket he was looking for to keep my MGS band safe, and then that was it for him. He just stood there: his eyes were almost closed, and he was all hunched over, barely standing upright. I grabbed a towel, lifted him out of the tub, set him on the counter, removed his perfectly yellow cape, and dried him off. I tried to wring out his cape as best I could, but it was still pretty wet, so I just draped it over the tub.

As I dried myself off, I looked over and saw that Maynard had lain down on the counter and was sound asleep. I carried him to my bed and slid him way under the covers so he could burrow in and get warm. As soon as my head hit the pillow, I felt Bunny jump up on the bed. She rooted her way under the covers, and I felt her curl up around Maynard.

Finally, we were home, but oddly I was having trouble falling asleep. It probably had something to do with the tremendous request that King Moo Moo and Queen Mee Mee had asked of me. And, it's probably normal that after traveling to an island somewhere in the South Pacific on the back of a Mystical Guiding Manatee, going through Time Warp Tunnels, meeting kings and queens, and swimming in the South Pacific Ocean, my mind would race. I'll just try and close my eyes for a minute and see if I can relax.

"Every strike brings me closer to the next home run"

- Babe Ruth -

Chapter Fifteen

*J*ake. Jake honey, wake up! Jake, wake up! Good grief son, you sleep like the dead! You're going to be late for school if you don't get up right now!"

"Gosh, Mom, why are you waking me up so early? I feel like I just fell asleep! Can I please sleep for just another hour or two?"

"Nope, not gonna happen! You know your dad's rule: if you're late for school, you can't go to practice. Up you go! Now, Jake! For goodness sake, why is your hair wet?" my mom asked, running her fingers through my hair. And why do you have your bathing suit on?" She yanked the covers off me.

"Uh, I don't know! Maybe I was sleepwalking again. You know I do that sometimes!"

"Well, it sure seems kinda weird! Anyway, you need to hustle; we're leaving in twenty minutes! And tonight you've really got to do something about this mess. This is ridiculous. Are these wet towels on the floor?" she asked as she bent over to pick them up. "You know I hate wet towels on the floor."

She was clearly starting to get annoyed with me as she walked into the bathroom to hang them up.

"Jake, what's this?"

Oh poop! I completely forgot I had draped Maynard's cape over the side of the tub to dry.

"Uh, what's what?" I asked as casually as I could.

"This!" she said as she came out of the bathroom with Maynard's perfectly yellow cape in her hand.

"Uh, gosh it looks like a yellow cape," I answered as I tried to quickly scooch past her and get into the bathroom.

"Yes, I can see that it's a cape. But to whom does this little cape belong?"

"Mom, I thought you said we were leaving in

twenty minutes. Can we worry about the cape later, please?"

"Well, I suppose, but things just seem a little weird: wet towels, wet hair, bathing suit, little cape. There's something about all of this that is vaguely familiar to me," I heard her mumble to herself as she left the room.

Thankfully she left Maynard's perfectly yellow cape on my bed, which I quickly grabbed and shoved under my covers down to where Maynard was sound asleep and then bolted to the shower.

A few minutes later, I ran out of my bathroom, having barely taken enough time to get dry and desperately looked for something clean to wear.

"Maynard, are you awake?" I asked, scurrying around my room trying to get all of my stuff together for practice and find all of my schoolbooks. I kept checking, but I didn't see any movement from under the covers. Oh my gosh, my homework. I didn't do any homework last night. Hopefully Kacey can help me out; thankfully she always does her homework. But I was still gonna have to do some serious cramming in the car on the way to school.

"Maynard, these trips to Kahwallawallapoopoo are gonna kill me! Hey are you awake?"

"Yeah, Jake, I'm awake, but barely! What's up?" Maynard replied from somewhere deep under the covers.

"Jake, how did I get in your bed and way down here under the covers? All I remember is popping up through the drain into your tub and feeling incredibly sleepy and freezing cold."

"Well, I put you down there, of course. You fell asleep on the counter, so I took off your cape, dried you off and tucked you in under the covers so you could get warm. And then dear, sweet Bunny jumped up on the bed, rooted her way under the covers, and snuggled up to you. She must have known you needed some love."

"I guess it must be those Mystical Guiding Manatee powers that attracts the ladies!" Maynard replied.

"Or, maybe she felt sorry for you because you looked like a drowned rat that was in desperate need of some attention," I teased.

"Maynard, can you come up here for a minute? I really need to talk to you."

"Yeah Jake, what's up? And why is my really cool cape all wadded up in a ball?" Maynard said as he slowly wiggled his way out from the nest he had made for himself under the covers.

"I don't have time to tell you why your cape is all wadded up in a ball; I'll tell you about that tonight when I get home. Maynard what I really want to tell you is that I had an amazing time last night. Meeting King Moo Moo and Queen Mee Mee, King Peetar, and Myrtle was probably the coolest thing that has ever happened to me. Probably even cooler than hitting that home run. I'm really happy that you're my Mystical Guiding Manatee, and I just want you to know that I've decided that I'm gonna do everything in my power to help bring baseball back to the Island of Kahwallawallapoopoo."

"Aw Jakey, you're gonna make me cry," Maynard teased.

"Come on, man!" I said. "I'm not kidding around. Your mom and dad asked for my help, and I want to honor their request. Besides, somehow my grandmother is involved in all this, and I want to find out more about what she knows and how everyone knows her. And then there's Kacey. I want her to come with us to the Island of Kahwallawallapoopoo one of these times so she can see for herself how cool everything is.

"Maynard, Maynard are you awake? Are you even listening to me?" I asked, as I tried to untangle him from my sheets.

"Yes, of course, I'm listening to you, Jake. I promise. I was just thinking about King Peetar. That was the first time I'd heard the entire story about how he lost his parents, and it just makes me so sad for him. Now that we're talking about it, I realize that we've got a lot of work to do. We're gonna need to make lots of trips to Kahwallawallapoopoo, and I'm just wondering how that's gonna happen. We've gotta find us a Guardian to help pull this off."

"I guess we'll just figure it out as we go along," I said, still trying to put all the pieces of the puzzle together in my head. "Hey, Maynard! I just remembered something. When I first told my grandmother about you, she asked me if I needed her to come out and help. At the time I wasn't sure what she meant; maybe she's known about this plan all along, and it was her way of telling me that she would be our Guardian and I should call her when I was ready. Holy cats, that completely blows my mind!" I yelled and started looking for my phone. "I've got to call my grandmother right now; I've just got to talk to her!"

"Jake, sit down, you're getting yourself all worked up and it's way too early in the morning to start making all of these plans," Maynard pleaded. "I'm sure we'll find out soon enough what Vicki-Lou knows or doesn't know, but what I do know for sure is if you don't get ready for school, right now, your mom is going to be smokin' mad at you. Let's call Vicki-Lou, I mean, your grandmother, tonight when you get home from practice. OK?"

"You're right, you're right," I said.

"Jake, can I please go back to sleep?" Maynard asked as he looked up at me with his big sleepy puppy dog eyes.

"Of course, Maynard! Go back to sleep, little buddy. I know you must be exhausted from our trip!"

"Yep, I'm pooped! Good night, Jake."

"Hey Maynard, can I ask you just one more question before you go back to sleep?"

"OK, Jake but please make it an easy question, I'm really, really sleepy!"

"Maynard, do you think King Peetar could have pitched in the major leagues?"

"Sadly, Jake, I guess we'll never know!" Maynard said with a sigh as he rolled himself back up into my sheets and drifted off to sleep.

"Well, Maynard, maybe we will; maybe we will!"

To Be Continued...

"Never let the fear
of striking out get in
your way."

- Babe Ruth -

Acknowledgments

Thank you, Christine for being so kind and gentle with me during those early days. Your edits helped me gain the confidence I needed to continue exposing my manuscript to more and more people. Your support and enthusiasm for the story and the characters was exactly what I needed to keep going.

Henry, we make the most unlikely of collaborators. It's fascinating to me because you're such a big, kind-hearted teddy bear with such an eccentric taste in so many things, especially all things related to comic books, haunted houses, and scary movies with lots of gore, yet you brought all my characters to life with such care and thoughtfulness. I'll never be able to thank you enough for taking on this challenge. The magic your pencils have created has brought me to tears on more than one occasion. Your ability to translate my words into this beautiful artwork continues to take my breath away. Your minute attention to detail is like the whipped cream on top of a perfect iced mocha. Thank you most of all for never getting frustrated with me when I asked you for just one more drawing and then just one more drawing and can you hurry because we are running out of time.

Thank you Anne-Marie, a busy mom of three, an awesome wife, and one heck of an amazing attorney. Thank you for taking the time in the middle of all that you have going on to write those all-important contracts for me. Of course, when I reached out to you I had already let too much time go by without having them prepared, but your kindness to put me at the top of your long list can never be repaid – well, come to think of it, maybe I could send more steaks, hamburgers, and hot dogs! Thank you again for being so gracious and generous with you time. I will always be grateful and thankful for your help.

Cindy, how does one begin to thank a person they

have known for fifty years? The list of silly, stupid, and crazy things we did along the way is certainly long and colorful and probably best left unmentioned. Of course, you've always been there when I needed you, but this time, for this project, you raised the bar from dearest friend to the person whose opinion I trusted most. Thankfully, your crazy analytical mind kept continuous watch for inconsistencies; if you hadn't been watching so diligently, the story would have been quite frustrating to the reader. But, most importantly I am grateful for your constant encouragement for me to engage myself more in the story-telling aspect of this project. Your enthusiasm for me to give you more details and to describe more of what was happening helped push me to creative places in my brain that I didn't know existed. Honestly, I know I could not have done this without you and I will never find enough ways to thank you.

To my sweet, silly, son Jake. You stole my heart the very minute the doctor handed you to me. This journey with you has brought immeasurable joy to my life and much laughter to my soul. The greatest gift I have ever received was to be your mom. I am so proud of all that you have become and so proud of all that you desire to be. Honestly, I wasn't sure how I was going to handle the transition once you left for college, so far, far away. It was the ultimate bittersweet experience. The only consolation was that you were doing exactly what we had raised you to do, to follow your dreams, yet so desperately not ready for that day to arrive. There were so many, many, many, tearful days but now look at us. These last two years watching you find your way and follow your dreams has transformed our relationship in ways I wasn't expecting. And then this project emerged, I'm still not sure from where, and you became one of my biggest fans. Thank you doesn't even begin to express how grateful I am for your constant support. It was wonderful how we seamlessly changed roles and you were there cheering me on and challenging me to raise the bar. Your encouragement to write it better, to take an idea further, to give the reader more, inspired me to want to do better and be better. I love you all the way to the moon....and back!

And finally, to my rock, my very best friend, my partner in all of our many business ventures, my husband of almost thirty years, Peter. Of all the people who supported me along the way, it was, without a doubt, your never-ending encouragement that kept me going. Your steadfast devotion in my ability when I had my moments of complete frustration that would sometimes spiral to despair in my confidence to actually pull this off is why I love you so much. I know you were relieved that I found a creative outlet for myself after Jake left for college but little did we know how much sacrifice this was going to be for you. We realized quickly that writing is a solo venture; it is truly remarkable how many hours of uninterrupted time is necessary for the creative process to happen. Thank you for graciously accepting that you would be spending so many evenings and weekends by yourself. And finally, I am especially grateful for all the times I would ask you to read and then re-read and then re-read again and again and again, section after section, and you would stop what you were doing and diligently read the pages I gave you and give me your feedback. It's been quite a journey we've been on all these years – p.h.!

Thank you Doug of Atlantic Publishing for venturing into an arena that was slightly uncharted for your company. I'll never forget sitting in your conference room explaining my story and showing you some of my characters, hoping I could encourage you to believe collaboration would be a really good idea; that I was in this for the long haul and was willing to do whatever necessary to ensure that this was a winning venture for both of us. I'm looking forward to many, many books published by Atlantic Publishing.

A very special thank you to Danielle. As my editor and chief guidance counselor, you have been tremendous. Your kindness and patience have been unwavering and I thank you for that. I am most grateful that you relentlessly urged me to give the reader more information and expand my ability to tell my story; looking back, I had written a screenplay, not a story, and now it's a story, thank you.

About the Author

Lisa Osgard lives in Jacksonville, Florida with her husband, their extremely spoiled beagle, and a cat named Shortstop. She loves traveling, reading, knitting, and most of all, watching her son play baseball and perform on the stage.

Website: www.kahwallawallapoopoo.com
Email: contact@kahwallawallapoopoo.com

About the Illustrator

Henry lives in Jacksonville, Florida with his significant other, his motorcycle, and his perilously large comic book collection. He is never without some sort of mark-making implement and a sketchbook. He happily draws pictures as often as possible – especially when offered treats or money to fund his comic book habit.

Email: honeygoblinart@gmail.com